HELP, PINK PIG!

HELP, PINK PIG!

C.S. Adler

G. P. Putnam's Sons
New York

Published by G.P. Putnam's Sons,
a division of The Putnam & Grosset Group,
200 Madison Avenue, New York, NY 10016.
Published simultaneously in Canada.
Printed in the United States of America.
Book design by Lisa Stokes.

Library of Congress Cataloging-in-Publication Data
Adler, C. S. (Carole S.)
Help, pink pig! / C.S. Adler.
p.   cm.
Summary: Moving to Los Angeles to live with her mother,
a lonely girl escapes the boredom and torment of
a neighborhood bully by entering a fantasy world
with her magical toy pig.
[1. Fantasy. 2. Mothers and daughters—Fiction.
3. Bullies—Fiction.] I. Title.
PZ7.A26145He 1990 [Fic]—dc20   89-34584 CIP AC
ISBN 0-399-22183-2

10   9   8   7   6   5   4   3   2   1
First Impression

*For Erna Adler, an admirable lady
whom it is my good fortune
to have as a mother-in-law*

one

The craziest thoughts went through Amanda's head as she walked out of the plane from New York through a sort of movable tunnel into the Los Angeles airport. What if she'd become invisible? Or if she'd landed on an alien planet? What if she didn't recognize Mother? Six months was a very long time. A stranger could claim to be her mother and kidnap her.

Pearly had had more sensible worries. "Now if your mother's not there, you just stay put and wait for her," Pearly had told Amanda, one of a long list of grandmotherly cautions. "If it didn't cost the world, I'd go with you," Pearly had said. "I never seen L.A., never been in a plane for that matter."

Amanda had never been in one either. "I'll write you, Grandma," she'd promised.

"You'd better. What am I going to tell them rabbits of yours if you don't write us?"

Then Pearly had cornered the flight attendant, in

whose charge she was leaving Amanda, and rattled on until the pretty young woman's smile wore out and Amanda got embarrassed. ". . . only eleven, small for her age, but sharp as a tack," Pearly had told the flight attendant. "She's been with me for the past six months while her Ma settled into a job in L.A. Now we got so used to one another, I hate to let her go." It was when Pearly had turned to tell Amanda, "Don't be too shy to ask when you need something," that Amanda saw the tears in her grandmother's eyes. Immediately, her own eyes filled up.

"Oh, Grandma, don't worry." Amanda squeezed Pearly's calloused hand hard.

"Awful sending a child clear across the country alone," Pearly had grumbled.

"She'll do fine. Kids do it all the time," the flight attendant chirruped. "Just you leave her to me and don't worry." Her polished nails touched Pearly's arm to signal her it was time to go, but Pearly didn't budge. The flight attendant flitted off.

"Grandma," Amanda said, "I'll come back and visit you soon."

"No, you won't." Pearly sniffled up her sadness. "It's too far. But I'm going to buy a lottery ticket, and if I win, you just bet I'll send you the fare."

"Or you could visit us and go to Disneyland with me."

"Better if you come to me." Pearly's voice sagged with despair, as if she expected they would never see each other again. She hugged Amanda hard. The flight attendant returned to warn Pearly that she wasn't supposed to be on the plane and had better leave now.

8

"Well, I'd best go or they'll take me for a stowaway," Pearly had said. Then she'd marched off without looking back.

Amanda had begun crying in earnest, which was how she came to miss experiencing the takeoff. Before she knew it, she was up above a lumpy sea of clouds. She'd been alert for the landing though, and already she found herself at the end of the tunnel where she saw people waiting for their friends and relatives to deplane.

There was Mother. No question it was her. She stood out even here in Los Angeles where everybody might be a movie star. Her dark hair was clipped and tilted sharply to one side, and her sapphire eyes shone above her high cheekbones, but it was the way she held herself that made her look so special.

"Amanda, oh, darling! You got here and you're all right. I had nightmares that something would go wrong." Mother embraced Amanda swiftly and even rocked her a little as if she really were delighted to see her. Then she stood back for the critical appraisal. As always, her eyes seemed to demand more than Amanda had to give. But all Mother said was, "Well, what do you have to say?"

"Hi."

"That's it? After all these months, just 'hi'?"

"Well," Amanda began, but then her mind went blank the way it used to when Mother was waiting for her to say something charming or funny or clever—like Dale, Amanda's big brother, might.

"Never mind. I'm just teasing you. I have a surprise," Mother said. "Look behind that post, Amanda."

Somehow Amanda guessed it was Dale, and before she'd taken two steps toward the post, he stepped from behind it in his army uniform, looking so handsome and so old. He lifted her as if she were weightless and hugged her tight.

"Dale! I'm so happy to see you. Oh, Dale, I missed you and missed you," Amanda cried.

"Me too, Mouse. I'm not even supposed to be here. I'm late getting back to the base, but I don't care if they punish me. I just had to say hi and give you a hug." He drew back, grinning and said, "You haven't changed one bit. Are you glad to be here?"

"Uh-huh." She clung to his hand. "Will I see you a lot now?"

He laughed. "Afraid not. But the next leave I get, I'm spending with you no matter what. Meanwhile, we'll just keep on writing each other. Okay?"

"Okay."

"Dale," Mother said. "You may not get your next leave if you're too late getting back."

"Right," Dale said. "Listen, you two take good care of each other, and I'll see you both in a few weeks." He kissed Mother, and then he kissed Amanda and squeezed her and took off at a run.

Amanda was bewildered. "Why was it so short?" she asked.

Mother raised an eyebrow. "He spent his time in L.A. with that girl he's involved with. I didn't even know he was here until he called me just before I left for the airport. If you hadn't been coming in, I doubt he'd have let me know he was in town at all."

Mother sounded so hurt that Amanda didn't ask any

10

more questions about Dale. Instead, she said, "I saw so many swimming pools, like blue eyes everyplace, when the plane was landing."

"Lots of people in L.A. have pools," Mother said. She took Amanda's hand and led her into the stream of people heading down the center aisle of the airport toward the baggage return. "And did you notice how different the mountains are?"

"Well, they're sort of bony," Amanda offered uncertainly.

"Bony and bare," Mother said, smiling as if Amanda had gotten that one right, at least. "Did you enjoy the flight?"

"Yes. I watched the movie, except I couldn't figure it out very well because I couldn't hear the words." She swung out of the way of a family burdened with bulging carry-on luggage. "Deaf people must have a hard time understanding things."

"I suppose . . . Didn't Pearly give you any spending money?"

"Sure. Oh, you mean about the movie? Well, the lady with the earphones went by so fast." Amanda thought of her other failure, the bland chicken that would have tasted better if she'd realized in time that the salt and pepper was hidden in tiny squares of rippled paper. She'd better not mention that or Mother would think she was stupid for sure.

Mother straightened Amanda's long fine brown hair as they walked. Oops! Amanda had meant to brush it before they landed, but in her excitement she'd forgotten.

"What we'll do first thing tomorrow is get your hair

11

styled," Mother said. "I found a fabulous stylist. She'll make you into a glamorous western girl so that you'll fit right in here. Then afterward, I'll take you straight to your new school. You won't mind starting immediately, will you?"

For Mother to ask if Amanda minded something was new, and it pleased her so much that she slid right by the worry about being transformed into a western girl. "It's all right," Amanda said. "You didn't get time off?"

"Well, I know I wrote you I was taking vacation days so that we could be together and I could show you around L.A., but my boss asked me to hold off. We're so busy right now. I just took half a day. We can plan a really special vacation for later. All right?"

"Sure," Amanda said quickly. "I'm just glad to be with you."

"Did you miss me, darling? Really?" Mother stopped short. "I was beginning to think you were happier with Pearly than you'd ever been with me. I'm sure she thought everything you did was wonderful. And all those animals she has . . . How can I compete?"

Amanda's heart did a little bounce step. "You're my mother," she said.

"Well, so I am, aren't I?" Mother stopped midstream and let the people flow around them while she gave Amanda a real kiss.

Just as she'd dreamed! Mother seemed glad to have her here. Maybe it would be different between them now. Amanda hoped so.

Mother drove expertly through the canyons of Los Angeles on the endless freeways she'd described in her letters, drove and drove until Amanda began to wonder. "Are we still in Los Angeles, Mother?"

"This new apartment I found is a ways out. Apartments are unbelievably expensive in L.A., and hard to find, but this one is actually more spacious than our little house in Schenectady was. And guess what, Amanda, you've got your own room."

"I know," Amanda said. "You wrote me."

"Did I?" Mother sounded dampened.

"I'm really glad," Amanda hastened to say.

Mother kept her eyes on the road. "Yes, and there's a garden out back, but you'll have to make friends with the landlady's daughter if you want to use it. We're on the second floor. We have a balcony though."

Amanda was quiet. Mother asked how she was feeling. "Fine," Amanda said. Then Mother asked how Pearly was, and Amanda said fine again.

"And school's fine too, I suppose." Mother's sharp tone clued Amanda that she'd overused the word. Ask about her job, Pearly had suggested when Amanda had worried out loud that she wouldn't have anything to talk about with Mother.

"How's your job going?" Amanda asked.

"Well, I still have it," Mother said. "I ought to find something better, I suppose. Tony says—did I write you about Tony?"

"No."

"Well, aren't you going to ask me about him?"

"Who is he?" Amanda obliged by asking.

"He's a handsome young sales rep, way younger than me, Amanda, but he's smitten. He calls me every night

13

and takes me to the most posh restaurants. Tomorrow night we'll both go out to dinner with him. Isn't that super?"

"Super," Amanda agreed and hoped it would be. Tony, Amanda thought. He must be the reason Mother was looking so lively and young. Back in Schenectady Mother had only had acquaintances to go to concerts and lectures with occasionally. Amanda drifted off, too tired to concentrate on Mother's description of a restaurant she'd been to with Tony. Pearly had been right when she had advised Amanda to sleep on the plane. Mother liked perky people. Dale was perky, "the Charmer" Mother used to call him. He would have kept the conversation going if he'd been able to stay with them. Dale could talk to anybody.

"Have you met Dale's girlfriend, Mother?" Amanda asked when Mother finished talking.

"Not yet. He told you about her?"

"He wrote me that she makes him laugh."

"He spends all his free time with her. I hope he's not getting too involved. Eighteen is too young for a serious relationship, and she certainly doesn't sound like the right girl for him."

"Why not?"

"She's a waitress, Amanda, not a college girl waiting tables, a real waitress."

No, Mother hadn't changed, Amanda thought, neither outside nor in. She still looked down her nose at anything ordinary, the way she'd looked down at Pearly who was a janitor. But Pearly was the best person Amanda knew, besides Dale. A little knot of resistance hardened in Amanda.

"Well, here we are. Home. Voilà." Mother gestured grandly.

Amanda was startled by the sudden appearance of a house. Weren't they still on the freeway? She craned her neck and saw it looming above them. They made a quick turn onto a narrow road and Mother pressed a button over her head. A garage door rolled up, and they drove into a dim space whose walls were hung with garden tools. Part of the garage was a staircase with a door at the top. Another door at ground level was at the other side of the back wall.

Mother led the way upstairs. "It's not a very pretty entrance," she said, "but it's private at least, and wait till you see the rooms."

"Where are the other houses, Mother? I mean, is this the only one around?"

"Yes, we're off by ourselves here. The only thing is, I don't want you walking out alone. The freeway traffic exits so fast that it's not safe. But nobody walks in L.A. anyway."

"Not even kids?" Mother's lips thinned, and Amanda changed her meaning hastily. "I mean, is there a school bus?"

"Of course. It stops right at the house. Voilà," Mother said again, flinging open the door to a sunny living room splashed with vividly colored chairs and a couch, all large and standing in islands of space. "What do you think of it, darling?" Mother sounded so anxious that Amanda didn't have the heart to disappoint her.

"It's nice."

"Just nice?"

15

"Well, it's—it's not like Schenectady. Where's our old furniture?"

"I sold all my antiques when I moved in a month ago," Mother said briskly. "This is my style now, bold and simple."

Amanda thought with regret of all the curved-leg tables and chairs and the netsuke collection. "It's nice," she repeated.

Mother groaned.

"Colorful," Amanda amended. But she could tell by Mother's expression that she'd failed again. They hadn't been together much more than an hour, and already Amanda was failing. She walked to the nearest window and looked out so that Mother wouldn't see her panic.

Garden? All Amanda saw was a vast valley of houses spilling out on impossibly steep hillsides. The valley was split by a road with toy-sized cars zipping along it in opposite directions. On the other side of the road, the land rose again less steeply. On that side the houses clustered in little neighborhoods of streets. Brown bone mountains hovered beyond that. "You said there was a garden."

"Not that way, silly. Over here where the balcony is." Mother drew back white fabric blinds and stepped out onto a balcony filled with plants and a pair of white chairs. Amanda joined her. She saw two children below in a garden.

"The girl's our landlady's daughter. Her name's Angel," Mother murmured. "The little boy's living with them while his parents are out of town. Shall I take you down to meet them?"

16

"I'm sort of tired," Amanda said apologetically.

"Of course you are, poor baby. I'll get supper on the table, and then you can go straight to bed. There'll be plenty of time to meet them. They're the only kids around for you to play with. . . . It's pretty, isn't it? The garden?"

"Very pretty," Amanda said. It was. Amazing orange and blue flowers, like birds, rose from a clump of spearlike leaves. A cascade of roses fell from a trellis along one high wall, and in between were bushes and beds of red and yellow flowers. A tree shaded one corner and grass carpeted the middle. The garden was inviting, but Amanda was more interested in the children.

They looked about her age, eleven. Maybe the downy-haired boy with his peachy cheeks and little nose was younger, but not by much. They were playing a board game. Amanda couldn't see which one. The girl was large with springy black hair, a broad face and pouty mouth. She reached out suddenly and gave the boy's arm an Indian burn. "Ow," he protested and jumped up holding his arm protectively. "What'd you do that for, Angel? I can't help if I'm winning."

The girl leaned over the board toward him and held up a threatening finger. "You can't win anything, Robbie Morrison. You can't win anything from me."

He hesitated only a second before sitting back down. He was still nursing his arm as they resumed their game.

Amanda shuddered. No way would she be friends with that girl. As if she could hear the thought, Angel looked up. She studied Amanda on the balcony and

17

smiled. Like a cat spotting its prey, Amanda thought and stepped back into the living room out of the line of sight. What was she going to do without anyone here to play with? School. But if you had to drive everywhere, and Mother was at work all day . . . Something splintered and stung in Amanda. She longed to run back to her grandmother who thought she was wonderful, her grandmother who rained love on her from an endless supply.

"Mother," Amanda called in desperation. "Do you still have Pink Pig?"

"Who?" Mother asked from the small, bare kitchen.

"Pink Pig. Remember, I sent her to you for Christmas so you wouldn't be lonely?"

"Oh, yes, of course." Mother had to think. The thinking made Amanda nervous. If anything had happened to Pink Pig . . . But finally Mother said, "It's somewhere on my dresser, maybe on that tray where I leave my rings."

"Is it okay if I look?"

"Amanda, what a question. This is your home."

Amanda nodded politely and said, "I'll set the table in a minute." She went to find her beloved miniature, the friend who'd helped her through the long, empty hours when she was waiting for Mother to get back from her bank job in Schenectady.

The shiny rose quartz creature was there, her mite-sized eyes as black as ever. She was lying on her side in a mess of pins and paper clips on top of a key chain.

"It's me," Amanda said as she held Pink Pig in the palm of her hand. "I'm here, Pink Pig," she said when nothing happened.

18

The glassy miniature didn't change. Had Amanda grown too old for the magic? Her eyes filled. "Pink Pig, it's me. I missed you. Come back," she begged. How could Pink Pig be gone? Amanda carried the figurine to her mother.

"Is it okay if I take Pink Pig back, Mother? I mean, if you don't want her that much?" ·

"Tell me," Mother said. "Why does it mean so much to you? Is it because Pearly gave it to you?"

Partly, Amanda thought, but Mother wouldn't want to hear that. "Because Pink Pig was magic. I mean, I used to think she was when I was younger."

"Magic," Mother's frown faded and she looked less tense. "We could use some, couldn't we? You keep your miniature, honey. Maybe the magic will come back for you."

Yes, Amanda thought, she needed Pink Pig. She needed some way to escape this big sunny cage.

The first thing Amanda took out of her suitcase was her miniature box. She removed a clown picture Mother had hung next to her bed and set the sectioned-off box on that hook. Then she unpacked all her precious miniatures and put them into their niches, along with Pink Pig. There were Frog, Ballerina, the corn husk dolls, Spangled Giraffe, Peasant Man and Peasant Woman, the knights—except that the Viking knight had been lost when she took it to school for social studies, and now there was a wooden knight with a beard Dale had sent her instead. She'd told him about the Viking being lost but hadn't mentioned that she didn't much care for knights and could have used a princess. She had no princesses on the shelf. Most of

19

the spaces were filled with miniature birds and flower vases.

Having her shelf set up comforted Amanda. It made the room seem more hers. Gently she stroked Pink Pig and whispered, "Hi, my friend," but Pink Pig remained small and cold. It might be the magic didn't work in California. That might be what was wrong. Amanda sighed and began to unpack the rest of her things.

two

The hairstylist was frightening. She looked to Amanda like the wicked witch from a modern day Snow White with her electrified hair and mask of makeup. "I like myself the way I am," Amanda got up the courage to tell Mother while they were waiting on the lipstick-colored chairs.

"Don't you want to fit in with the other girls in your class?"

Fitting in was Amanda's talent. She could blend into a group so well nobody even noticed her. "But Mother," Amanda persisted, "looking weird'll make me stand out, not fit in."

"Oh, Amanda, trust me. You'll see. . . . We also need to buy you some new outfits," Mother decided after giving Amanda a slow critical once-over.

Amanda sat up straight. "Pearly already bought me lots of new stuff. I was wearing a new outfit when I came yesterday."

"Were you?" Mother tried to remember. "You mean that pink tee shirt and those elastic-banded pants?"

"Pearly thought you'd like pink."

"How would Pearly know? But *you* certainly should remember your mother's favorite color. It's turquoise." Mother sounded frosty. "Or are you so infatuated with that grandmother of yours that you've forgotten your mother's tastes?"

Amanda's fingers gripped the seat of the red plastic chair. She knew her mother's tastes. She knew that Mother was proud of her son's looks and disappointed by her daughter's plainness. Dale looked like Mother, but Amanda looked like herself. At least that was what Pearly had told her when Amanda had asked if she looked like her father. In the mirror herself was small, even featured, and pale.

Mother's face puckered. "I suppose you're still angry that I left you. That's it, isn't it? Let's start being honest with one another, Amanda. Say so if you're mad at me. Say so, and we'll talk about it."

"I wasn't angry. I knew you had to go when the bank—when you had that trouble, and I *wanted* to stay with Pearly and my friends at school, remember? But I don't want to be done over now, Mother." Amanda watched Mother's face anxiously. Disagreeing with her was risky.

Mother's lips lifted in a wry smile. "In other words, you were happy with Pearly, and if I push you too hard, you'll run back to her. Right?"

It was so right and so wrong that Amanda didn't know what to say. "You're my mother," she tried cautiously. "I've really been looking forward to being with you."

Mother's eyes glazed with tears, and her voice went high as she said, "I want us to be close, Amanda. I don't know how to reach you, but I want us to be close."

Amanda's heart was drumming so loudly she couldn't think. Instead, she squeezed Mother's hand. To her relief, that seemed to help.

"All right," Mother sighed. "All right." Her voice became teasing. "I'll tell Celeste to leave you a tad mousy, if that's what you want."

"Thank you," Amanda said.

Actually, although she didn't look like the old straight-haired Amanda once Celeste got through giving her a permanent, Amanda did think the girl in the mirror was appealing, almost pretty in fact. Celeste had finished by touching up her lips with color and darkening her eyelashes. Besides, the new face looked well in the clothes Mother bought to go with it, mix-and-match tops and a skirt and pants in a shiny store where the salesgirls dressed like dolls in the same crayon-colored mix-and-match clothes.

"What do you think?" Mother asked. She was standing behind Amanda looking at her expectantly in the dressing room mirror.

Mother's face was beautiful in the mirror. Amanda's gaze slid reluctantly to the small girl with the mass of curly hair below and to the right of Mother. "I think I look more like your daughter now," Amanda said wistfully.

23

"Oh, darling." Mother hugged her from behind. "I do love you so much."

"I love you, too," Amanda said, but her voice sounded thin. It didn't vibrate with true feeling. It usually didn't.

They drove to school next. It was a plain, low building with a lot of windows surrounded by grass, a playground, and a ballfield. When Mother was ready to leave Amanda with the guidance counselor, she asked doubtfully, "Will you be all right, darling?" Amanda gave her a smile to take away with her.

"Don't worry about coming in so late in the year," the guidance counselor advised Amanda. "The way kids come and go around here, you'll find plenty of others who are new." She was plain-faced and plainly dressed. Amanda liked her.

"I'm not scared," she said.

"Fine. And your records show you're a solid B student. You shouldn't have *any* trouble. But come see me and let me know how you're doing anyway, okay?" She looked sincerely interested.

"Yes," Amanda said. "Thank you." She followed the guidance counselor down a hall just like the one in Amanda's old school except for the red tile on the walls. The classroom they entered seemed familiar, too, and so did the brown, black, and blond heads bent over desks. The only sound was the soft scurrying of pencils on paper.

The young teacher, Miss Blount, looked up from her desk in front of the room and greeted Amanda pleasantly. Then she whispered, "We're in the middle of a timed math test. I'll introduce you to the class later. . . . Would you like to sit there in the back or over by the window?"

"The window, please," Amanda said.

A minute later she was comfortably fitted into place and paging through the books Miss Blount had given her. "Don't worry if you don't understand the material," Miss Blount said. "I'll go easy on you so long as you try."

Amanda didn't see anything in the math book that was new to her, and the health book was the same one she'd been using in New York. Apparently all she had to do for reading was a report on a book of her choice. Since she always had a book in hand to read, that was no problem. So far, so good.

She turned her attention to her classmates and began sifting through for possible friends, a best friend like Libby if possible. A small, red-haired girl in the front row was chewing her pencil and squirming in her seat. Suddenly she looked over at Amanda and crossed her eyes clownishly. Amanda smiled. The girl smiled back. Amanda relaxed. She would have someone to talk to in school, at least.

She got off the school bus on the empty hill that sheered off to one side and rose up to the steep embankment of the overpass on the other. One good thing about theirs being the only house was that she couldn't miss it. Mother had given her a key to let herself in. Amanda was used to being alone after school. Mother had always worked, leaving her with a babysitter until that lady moved away, and later leaving Amanda in

Dale's care. He hadn't been a very faithful sitter. Often he'd hung out with his friends instead of coming home, but he'd been a good brother nevertheless because he'd loved her just as she was. Little Mouse he'd called her fondly. Dale had joined the army after Mother had to quit her job and leave town. Amanda hoped his next leave came soon.

She took her glass of milk to the balcony and drank it, looking down into the garden. A lady was weeding a bed of red flowers. She got up to carry off a basket of weeds, and then she just stood there like a statue with the basket on her hip. What could she be thinking to stand there so long, Amanda wondered.

"Ma, you didn't get the right cookies again. I told you the soft kind. Can't you remember anything?" It was Angel's voice coming from inside the house. Already Amanda recognized it.

"I'm sorry, Angel." The big woman looked like Angel, but her voice was soft. "I'll get you the right ones tomorrow."

"You never get anything right," Angel complained. "I wish Dad'd get home."

The woman's eyes glazed with tears, but she didn't say anything, just bent her head and toted the basket of weeds away. Amanda felt sorry for her and wondered if she was crying because of the way Angel talked to her. Nasty, Amanda thought. Angel was a nasty girl.

Pink Pig was in her cubbyhole on the miniature shelf where Amanda had left her. Or was she really in the Little World snoozing happily in the sunshine there? Hopefully, Amanda kissed her, but nothing hap-

26

pened. Probably, Amanda told herself again, Pink Pig only could come to life on the East Coast. Probably her magic was local.

Mother had made the bedroom really pretty for her, Amanda realized now. She liked the white painted furniture and the flower-sprigged curtains and bedspread. In Pearly's patched-together house, Amanda had slept with the sewing machine and mismatched everything. Her chair had stuffing pushing out through holes in it. Even so, she missed that old bedroom. It had wrapped itself around her like Pearly's comforting presence.

Pearly. Amanda got out the box of unicorn writing paper Mother had sent her for her birthday and began composing a letter to her grandmother.

"I miss my room and the rabbits and kittens and you," Amanda wrote. "Don't forget it's Flopsy that likes spinach leaves and Mopsy gets the carrot tops. School's okay. Mother got me a haircut, but she liked the new outfit you bought me." Amanda wrote the small lie easily, knowing it would make Pearly happy. Pearly had paid for the pink pants and shirt with her own money, and she didn't earn a lot as a custodian in the school Amanda had attended.

Amanda finished the letter with a drawing of Pink Pig and exes for kisses. "Lots of love," she wrote and tucked the letter into an envelope. Tonight she'd ask Mother for a stamp.

The book Amanda was reading was one of a series by Stephanie Tolan about the adventurous Skinner family. It would do fine for her book report, she decided.

She took both the book and Pink Pig to the balcony and settled down to read.

A few minutes later she heard Angel yell, "You come out here. Come out here, Robbie."

Amanda watched the sweet-faced boy amble into the garden. He was a head shorter than Angel, and puny beside her solid body. "Catch," Angel said and tossed a baseball at him.

He fumbled it, and she scoffed, "Come on. You got to learn to catch a ball at least."

"I want to finish my drawing first," Robbie said.

"No, you don't. Now, catch." The ball came harder. Again he missed it.

"You better try, Robbie Morrison. Try or you'll be sorry."

"I am trying, Angel. I'm just not good at ball games."

"You're not good at anything."

"Yes, I am."

"What? Drawing and reading? That's sissy stuff. Catch."

This time he caught the ball in the stomach. He grunted as if it hurt, but then, without complaining, he dropped to his hands and knees and crawled under the bush where the ball had rolled.

"Woof woof," Angel said. "If you won't play ball, you can be my dog. That's what you look like in that bush. Come here little doggy, come here." Screeching, Angel knocked Robbie flat and began to tickle him.

"Cut it out," Robbie begged. "Stop, Angel. Please."

Amanda couldn't see what Angel was doing to the boy except that she wasn't leaving him alone. He began to sound desperate as he pleaded with her to let him be.

"Stop!" Amanda called without thinking. Angel looked up. Amanda drew back where she couldn't be seen. Then she took her book and Pink Pig and curled up in a corner of the couch feeling miserable. She ached for Pearly. She missed her friends. Los Angeles was awful and she hated it.

On the couch with her book, Amanda felt something hard poke her hip. She picked Pink Pig out of the cushion.

"You should've told that mean kid off," Pink Pig said.

"What?"

Pink Pig glowed with indignation. "Why didn't you tell her to leave him alone?"

"She wouldn't have listened to me," Amanda said.

"Two against one," Pink Pig said.

"You think I should help him?"

"Somebody should," Pink Pig said.

"You and me?" Amanda asked.

"Together. Like when we fought the wizard."

"I'm so glad to have you back," Amanda said. "Why didn't you come last night when I asked you?"

"You sent me away, Amanda. You said you didn't need me anymore."

"Well, I do need you now more than ever." Just feeling Pink Pig's warm, rubbery body alive in her hands cheered Amanda up considerably.

Mother was neon lighted with excitement when she walked in. "Put on the new skirt with that top,

Amanda. My friend, Tony Horton, is taking us out to dinner."

"He's your boyfriend?" Amanda asked.

"Yes. Be your most charming self tonight for my sake, darling. He says he's not much for children. I told him you were forty years old when you were born."

"I'm eleven, Mother."

"Are you?" Mother teased. "You act older than me. Anyway, hurry. He's calling for us in half an hour."

It only took Amanda five minutes to wash her face and hands, cut the tags off her new skirt and put it on. She even shook her hair into place the way Celeste had showed her. But when she looked in the mirror she grew doubtful. Charming? Even her new self looked doubtful. She was Little Mouse, good but boring. Taking a deep breath, Amanda tried on a smile. She would do her best for Mother's sake.

An hour later, Mother was fidgeting over the tray of cocktail tidbits she'd arranged. She'd filled the ice bucket and set out glasses and a bottle of scotch which she said was Tony's drink. She touched her hair. "How do I look?"

"You always look beautiful, Mother."

That earned a hug. "Thanks, baby." Mother touched the shadowy pockets under her own eyes and went to look in the bathroom mirror which was surrounded with a ring of lights. "Amanda," she called. "You let him in when he comes. Tell him I'll be right there."

"Okay." Out of range of Mother's nervous vibrations, Amanda was able to pick up her book and slip into it. She'd finished two chapters when the phone rang. Mother was in the bedroom now. Amanda answered the phone.

"Hi. This is Amanda. Who's this, please?"

"Tony Horton. Let me speak to your mother, kid."

"Okay. Just a minute." He'd sounded impatient, Amanda thought, and not very polite. No "hello" and no "may I, please."

Amanda tried not to listen to the conversation, but she couldn't help hearing the anxious chiming of Mother's voice, and it didn't surprise her to learn that they weren't going out to dinner after all.

Afterward, Mother explained. "He had to work late. What say you and I go out for a bite to eat somewhere?" She put on a pretend smile to hide how bad she was feeling. "What would you like?"

"Pizza?"

"How about Chinese?" Mother countered.

"Okay." It was mean of Mother's friend to disappoint her so badly. Amanda felt sorry enough for her to eat anything to please her. So far it didn't look as if Mother was having such a good time in L.A. either.

three

While they were waiting for their spareribs and Moo Goo Gai Pan at the Chinese restaurant, Mother asked Amanda how her first day at the new school had gone.

"Fine," Amanda answered without thinking.

Mother eyed her critically and said, "You know, Amanda, if you'd talk to me, if you'd share a few thoughts, we might manage to have a real conversation someday."

"Oh." Amanda tensed with the effort of digging up a thought that might interest Mother. "Well," she offered finally, "there's a girl named Megan in my class who's new here, too. She's got red hair and she's sort of funny. We sat together at lunch."

"Where's she from?"

"I didn't ask her."

Mother raised an eyebrow. "Why not? And what do you mean, 'sort of funny'?"

"Oh, she's always making faces."

"She doesn't sound very bright. Be careful she doesn't get you in trouble."

Amanda looked at her hands which were gripping each other in her lap. Well, she'd expected Mother to shoot down her news. As to getting into trouble, she'd rather chance that than sit alone at lunch.

"And your teacher?" Mother asked.

"Miss Blount? She seems okay. She said she'd introduce me, but then she forgot."

"Young?"

"Umm hum."

Mother clicked her long fingernails on the table for a while. Then she muttered, "I don't know why Tony even said he'd take us out to eat if he was going to change his mind."

"Maybe he didn't know he had to work late."

"He's always working late. It's probably just an excuse. Last week I bought expensive concert tickets because he claimed he wanted me to educate him in classical music, and then he didn't go."

"Do you like him a lot, Mother?"

Mother clicked her fingernails some more. "Sometimes I do. Sometimes I wonder what's gotten into me. I had such high standards, and now—"

A silence fell upon them then. Amanda was relieved when the waiter brought their food which gave them something safe to chat about while they ate.

As soon as they got home, Mother said she had a headache and went to her room. Amanda retreated, too, with Pink Pig and her book.

"Let's go visit the Little World," Amanda said. She

33

remembered the last time she'd been there and how happy everyone had been. "I can't wait to get back."

"It's changed a lot," Pink Pig warned her. "With Wizard gone, the knights took over the castle. Dark Knight drove the Viking away and rules the people now."

"Is he a good ruler?" Amanda asked uneasily, recalling the fierce look of the pewter knight whose helmet hid his face.

"In some ways he's worse for the people of the Little World than Wizard ever was."

"Oh, no." Amanda was sorry to hear that. "I thought when we got rid of Wizard, the Little World would stay happy."

"Would you want to help make it that way again?" Pink Pig asked.

"I don't know if I can," Amanda said. "I don't know if I can help anyone when I can't even help myself." She thought of her mother who wasn't happy, and Robbie.

"Let's try," Pink Pig urged.

To please her friend, Amanda agreed. "But not tonight," she said. Tonight she needed a rest from trouble. Mother hadn't been the only one disappointed today.

* * *

In the morning Mother seemed depressed. Her voice was heavy as she said, "I'll pick up some fish for our dinner." She gave Amanda lunch money and asked her to get a salad ready when she got home from school. Fish and salad was Mother's favorite menu. It kept her

34

as thin as she liked to be, but Amanda didn't mind. She didn't eat much anyway.

School had no surprises. When Amanda asked Megan where she came from, she said Chicago. They were sitting with their trays touching across the table from each other in the cafeteria.

"Chicago's a great city. I never even heard of Schenectady," Megan said.

"It's in upstate New York. I liked it there."

"Little cities are boring," Megan said. "I lived in one once and there wasn't anything to do."

"There was lots to do in Schenectady."

"Like what?"

"Well, my grandmother has rabbits and kittens. I lived with her the last few months, and I helped her take care of the animals and her yard. We dug up a vegetable garden and built a shed."

"What about friends?"

"And I went on bike rides with my friends and to parks, and my best friend Libby and I had sleep-overs at each other's houses."

"Boring. In Chicago my Dad and me belonged to this health club, and I did gymnastics and swam and stuff there. And weekends we went to the zoo. I love zoos."

"There isn't any zoo in Schenectady."

"My mother lives in Chicago, too, but I didn't see her much. She and my father split. Are you split?"

"Sort of. It's just Mother and me, now my brother's in the army."

"Really?" Megan looked pleased. "Maybe we could

get our parents together. Is your mother as pretty as you?"

"I'm not pretty," Amanda said.

"Well, you have a straight nose, and your hair looks like honey. My hair's like red wires and my nose is a stub."

"I think you look nice," Amanda said.

"For a clown." Megan made her eyes cross. "Even my father calls me Monkey."

"My brother calls me Mouse," Amanda offered as consolation. The truth was Megan did look a little like a red-headed monkey, so small and wiry with a face that never kept still.

"I wish I had a brother," Megan said.

After lunch Amanda stood looking at herself in the mirror in the girls' room. "Pretty," Megan had said. Did the permanent really make her pretty? No, her solemn old self was still there. Just the surface was new. She was Amanda in disguise.

With three hours to go until Mother got home from work, Amanda finished her book, then idled over to the balcony to see what was going on in the garden. Robbie was sitting on the lawn facing her and drawing. He was alone today. Amanda waited for him to say something because he kept looking right at her and smiling to himself, but he worked in silence. She wondered if he could be smiling because Angel wasn't around.

"Hi," Amanda called to him at last. He had a sweet face, a boy doll face.

"Don't move," he said. "I'm drawing you."

"Me?"

36

"Yes, you're the princess in the tower. Only I'm giving you long straight hair. Princesses are supposed to have long hair. Do you want dark or light?"

Amanda thought about it. Mother's black hair was a wonderful surprise with her blue eyes, but Amanda's eyes were the color of mud. "Any color that goes with the picture," she said.

He stopped drawing and looked at her with interest. "Do you like to do art, too?"

"I can't draw."

"Everyone can draw. It's just if you like to, you're better at it."

"Can I see your picture?"

"Sure." He brought the drawing pad over and stood as close as he could get under the balcony.

"It's hard to see from here," she said.

"I could come up to show you, or you could come down." He thought about it. "She'll probably get home soon. She's shopping with her mother. I better come up."

Amanda didn't have to ask who "she" was. He sounded different without Angel around, more confident and lively. He disappeared into the house and in a minute was knocking a one-three-two rhythm on her door.

"Hi," he said when Amanda let him in. "I'm Robbie." He thrust the pad at her.

Amanda was amazed. The drawing looked like something out of a book of fairy tales. Of course, the princess didn't resemble her at all. "I'm Amanda," she said.

"A-mann-da," he repeated, making it sound musical. "That's a good name for you."

They both heard the garage door and tensed. "They're home," Robbie said.

Amanda was disappointed. "You have to go, huh?"

"What for? I hate Angel. It's a whole month since my parents left me here so my mom could do her internship at the hospital and my dad could study Chinese at the institute, and Angel's only been nice to me one day. You know which? The first day because my parents were still around. The minute they left she turned into a monster."

"But won't Angel's mother wonder where you are?"

"Moira won't care. I'll tell her I took a walk."

"Where?"

"Nowhere. I'll say I walked up the ramp to the freeway and down the island in the middle. That'll scare her, and she'll tell me not to, and I'll promise I won't because who'd want to walk on that freeway anyway?"

"Would Angel's mother believe you'd do that?"

"Moira'll believe anything. She's a poet. Out there somewhere." He gestured at the sky outside the window. "Anyway, danger doesn't bother me." His grin was mischievous, watching her face for a reaction to his boast.

"It doesn't?" Amanda thought about how meek he had seemed with Angel.

"*You* don't believe me?"

"I just . . . I don't know." To avoid hurting his feelings, she steered the subject away from him. "I have a friend and we go on adventures, but I don't really *like* danger. I get scared easy."

"Me, too," Robbie admitted. He sighed. "I'm really kind of a coward, but I sure would like to be brave."

"You can be then," Amanda said. She had been, after all, when she'd had to be to get the wizard out of the Little World.

"You think so? When will it happen?"

"When the right time comes."

It sounded true to her as she said it, and he nodded as if she'd convinced him. Encouraged, she asked, "Robbie, if you hate Angel, why don't you get your parents to put you with some other family?"

He shoved his fist under his chin. "I wrote my mother about Angel, but Mom's busy. They keep her working like thirty-six-hour shifts taking care of patients. She's going to be a psychiatrist. And my dad, I don't even have a telephone number for the dorm where he's staying at this special institute. It's near San Diego someplace. We used to live in San Diego."

"So what did your mother say?"

"She didn't answer me." He frowned. "She's never not answered me, Amanda. I guess she's mad at me for complaining. She's big on being strong, and I'm not very."

"Can't you call her?"

He shook his head. "I tried. I called the hospital, but I couldn't get through to her. I'm not really supposed to call her when she's on duty. So I didn't tell them who I was."

"You could ask Angel's mother to call for you."

"Moira? She's so spacey. My mom says Moira was a talented poet. She even got stuff published when they were college roommates. That's how my mom knows

39

her, from college—but I don't see her writing anything. She just works in the garden or watches TV.
She doesn't even get our meals together until Angel
starts yelling that she's hungry."

"Is the father nice?"

"I don't know. My parents met him, and they
thought he was okay. Anyway, he's away. It's sort of
secret, I think. Maybe he's a C.I.A. agent or something."

"Well, anytime you want to escape from Angel, you
can come up here," Amanda offered.

"Thanks, I'll do that—if Angel lets me, I will. Hey,
you could do something for me."

"What?"

"Keep a key for me."

"Your key?"

"It's to the trunk where I keep my castle and
knights. They're my favorite thing, and Angel's always
trying to find where I hid the key so she can wreck my
knights. They're plastic, but they've got all kinds of
little parts—neat swords and shields and helmets. She
already stole one of them."

"You'd like the Little World if you like knights and
castles," Amanda said, thinking out loud. "My brother
just sent me a wooden knight. Want to see it?"

"Sure," he said. "Do you like knights and stuff?"

"Not really. Knights are boys' things."

"Joan of Arc was a knight."

Amanda looked at him.

"Well, she was."

"I like my little animals better."

She took him into her bedroom to show him the miniature shelf. Of all the figures on it, Robbie's favorite was the brown wooden knight. He also liked the dragon and the pewter horse and the helmeted pewter knight.

"What's the Little World?" Robbie asked her suddenly.

"What?" She'd forgotten that she'd mentioned it. Cautiously she said, "It's hard to explain. Maybe sometime I'll tell you about it." She meant when she knew him better, and if she trusted him not to think she was crazy. So far, Mother and Dale and even her friends in Schenectady who knew about the Little World thought she was crazy to believe in it. So far she didn't know anyone who wouldn't think she was crazy.

"Well, so will you hold my key?"

"Sure," Amanda said.

The crack of a pebble against glass startled them. They both turned toward the sliding glass door in the living room as another pebble smacked against it.

"I know you're up there, Robbie Morrison. You better come down before I get mad."

"It's Angel," Robbie whispered.

"What are you going to do?"

"I'll sneak downstairs and tell her I went for a walk. Could you keep her talking so she doesn't see me coming in?"

"I'll try." Amanda stepped onto the balcony and surprised herself by how coolly she spoke to the bulky girl below. "You better stop that before you break this window."

"What if I do? It's my window."

41

"And you'll have to get it fixed then, and that costs money."

At the mention of money, Angel dropped her arm. "You want to come down and play?" she said next.

"No, thank you."

"You've been playing with that Robbie, haven't you?"

"What do you care?"

Angel stared at her for a minute. Then she said, "Come down. I'll play whatever you want. You name it. I've got all the games."

"I have to make salad for my mother. She'll be home soon."

"Salad," Angel scoffed. "I have to make the sal-ad for my dear ma-mmy." She looked angry enough to spit. "You're a real priss. Who wants to play with you anyway!" She stomped off into her house. Amanda hoped Robbie had managed to get around to the right door.

She found Robbie's drawing pad on the table in the dinette. Tomorrow she'd slip it back to him. The drawing of the princess on the balcony wasn't the only one in the book. There was one whole page of very realistic looking knights, one page of a castle with flags flying, and a page where he'd tried, not too successfully, to draw horses. The knights and castles were done with loving detail.

Pink Pig came alive as soon as Amanda picked her up. "So what do you think of him?" Amanda asked her.

"He's nice."

"He's going to trust me with his key. Can I trust him back?"

"You mean, invite him into the Little World with us?"

"He might have some good ideas about this Dark Knight who's taken Wizard's place," Amanda suggested.

"Tell you what," Pink Pig said. "Introduce us next time he comes. When he holds me, I'll know if we can trust him or not."

It would be good if they could trust him, Amanda thought. It would be fun to have another companion in the Little World. And Robbie liked knights and castles. She could just imagine how impressed he'd be by Wizard's castle—if it was still as she remembered it, if Dark Knight hadn't ruined it. Now she really wanted to return and see.

four

Robbie was out in the garden with Angel. If Amanda returned his drawing pad to him now, Angel would guess where he'd been yesterday afternoon. What she'd better do, Amanda decided, was keep an eye on the garden while she read her new library book. Then if Angel happened to go indoors for a minute, Amanda could toss the pad down to Robbie.

Looking for something to protect it, Amanda found a stash of colorful plastic bags printed with the names of shops where Mother had bought things. She had always shopped to cheer herself up. Judging by the number of bags there, she had needed a lot of cheering up lately. Amanda wondered if grownups got as lonely as kids. Well, even if they did, they could do something about it. They weren't confined to an apartment, jailed for their own safety.

Angel had Robbie digging near the side wall of the garden. "This is the spot. I'm sure it is," Amanda heard Angel say.

"Nothing's here but dirt and tree roots, and I'm tired, Angel," Robbie complained.

"Digging's good for you. It develops muscles. And you sure need 'em."

"No, I don't. I'm too young for muscles."

"Too girly you mean. Dig, Robbie. I know that's where I buried my cat last year."

Amanda was startled. What did Angel want to do with a dead cat? The girl was awful. There had to be a way to pry Robbie loose from her, but how? Amanda went to consult with Pink Pig who was snoozing on the sunny windowsill in her bedroom.

Pink Pig yawned. "Are we going to the Little World now?"

"After I get Robbie away from Angel for a minute, but I don't know how to do it."

"Call her up and ask to borrow something," Pink Pig suggested.

"But I don't know her number."

"Wouldn't your mother have written it in her telephone book?"

"Right." Pink Pig had such good sense, Amanda thought. And Mother was efficient. The Delaneys' number was clearly written in the mostly empty book next to the phone.

Amanda had to let the phone ring several times before Moira Delaney finally answered. "May I speak to Angel, please?"

"Angel? Are you a friend of hers?" Moira asked.

"It's Amanda—from upstairs?"

"Oh, yes, Amanda. Your mother said you were coming. I was delighted when I heard you and Angel are

45

almost the same age," Moira gushed. "Why don't you just come down and join her in the garden? She's there with Robbie who's staying with us for a few months. He's a lovely boy, and I'm sure you'll like him."

Moira's delight that Angel had a friend calling her made Amanda feel guilty for not being a friend. She said awkwardly, "Well, but—I'd just like to ask Angel something over the phone, please."

"Oh . . . all right." Moira sounded disappointed. Amanda heard her put the receiver down and then her slow footsteps.

"Hi." Angel's voice was loud and clear. "What do you want?"

Amanda gulped. What did she want? She thought fast. "Do you have a map of California I could borrow? I need it for my homework."

"A map of California?" Angel repeated. "I don't think so. Hold it a sec and I'll look."

That was what she'd been hoping to hear. Amanda raced to the balcony. Robbie was lying on his back in the grass resting. "Robbie," she whispered as loudly as she dared.

He looked up.

"Here's your drawing pad. Catch." She dropped the plastic bag, and he picked it up and immediately tucked it under a bush. In a more normal voice she asked, "What's she want to dig up a dead cat for?"

"To see if it's a skeleton yet. If it's a skeleton, she's going to take it to school for science. I think I touched something with the shovel, but no way I'd tell her. I mean, what if it isn't a skeleton yet? Yuck."

"She'll be back in a minute. Do you want to come up here?"

"I better not. Nobody'd believe I went for a walk on the freeway two days in a row. . . . Amanda, you know, about the key? What if I wait until she's watching TV tonight, and I sneak upstairs? Or I could go to the garden and you could let down a string, and I tie the key to it?"

Amanda thought he was making it unnecessarily complicated but she said, "Anyway's fine with me."

Suddenly Angel was there. "What are you two talking about?"

"I was just telling Robbie that I need a map," Amanda lied quickly.

"Well, here it is." Angel held up a folded gas station map. "This one's my dad's so you better be careful."

"I'll lower a bag you can put it in," Amanda said.

"What for? Why don't you come down here and get it?"

"Well, I have to do my work," Amanda said.

"Oh, big deal. How much homework did they give you? You're only eleven, right? I'm twelve, and I don't get nothing. And Robbie, he's just a ten-year-old baby. He still gets recess." She laughed as if she'd made a joke.

"I'm in the same sixth-grade class as you," Robbie said to her.

"That's because they got mixed up because you came from that fancy-dancy program in San Diego. What grade are you in, Amanda?"

"Sixth."

"Huh," Angel said. "Well, I'd be in seventh except I stayed home too much last year."

"What for?"

"Nothing. I hate school, and my dad used to take me to the studio with him sometimes. He's an extra, and he was a stunt man, and he rode in rodeos even. He's going to get me a horse someday." A smile of pure joy wiped the meanness from her face.

Nevertheless, Amanda was glad that she wasn't in the same sixth-grade class as Angel. Poor Robbie had to deal with her all day in school and out.

"So are you coming to get this map, or should I put it back?" Angel asked.

"I'll come." Amanda hurried through the apartment and down the garage stairs and outside. Should she ring the front doorbell, or what? While she was standing there surveying the blank front of the house which continued into a high wall, she heard Robbie shouting in the garden.

"No, Angel, don't. Give it back to me. It's my only one."

Frantically, Amanda rang the doorbell.

Out of the corner of her eye she saw Angel's head appear above the stone wall. She had Robbie's sketch pad flapping in her hand.

"Come and get it," Angel said.

"Please, Angel," Robbie pleaded. "I'll draw your picture too."

"You better not. You'd make me look ugly. I know you."

"I'll draw anything you want."

48

"Come on, sissy. Climb up here and get your pad," Angel taunted. Her legs were spread apart for balance. Amanda held her breath in fear. Slowly, Angel began sidling around the corner. Amanda gasped. Now Angel was on the canyon side. If she fell, she'd be killed. Amanda banged on the door. Moira had to come. She just had to.

There was a scream. Amanda's heart stopped. The door opened. "I think Angel fell off the wall," Amanda cried.

"Angel!" Moira cried and went running through her apartment out the sliding door to the garden. Amanda followed on her heels through the dim living room in which the turned-on TV was the only bright object.

Angel was standing in the garden next to Robbie who was crying.

"What happened?" Moira asked. "She said you fell off the wall, Angel."

"Fell? Me?" Angel made it sound ridiculous. "I was just showing Robbie something." The drawing pad was gone.

"You scared me half to death," Moira chided Amanda, but gently. The sorrowful lines of her face could not look anything but gentle, Amanda thought. Even annoyed, Moira had a softness to her. Her daughter had her springy black hair and big bones, but Angel was finished in hard edges. "You children play nice now and don't climb on that wall. It's dangerous. Okay?" Moira smiled forgivingly at Amanda. "I'm sure you meant well, dear." She stepped back into the house.

49

Amanda turned to follow her.

"Don't you want the map?" Angel demanded.

"Did you throw Robbie's drawing pad off the wall?"

"What's it to you?"

"I think you're mean," Amanda said.

"Who made you Robbie's bodyguard? He drew you on the balcony, didn't he? He made you look like a princess. Boy, you sure pick dumb boyfriends."

"He's not my boyfriend."

"Then what'd he draw you for?"

She sounded jealous, Amanda realized. And angry. Calmly she said, "I don't want the map anymore. Thank you, anyway."

"Oh, ooh, 'thank you anyways' the princess says." Angel minced around in a circle with her hands flapping limply.

"Why don't you tell Mrs. Delaney Angel threw your pad away, Robbie?" Amanda asked.

Angel laughed meanly. "She wouldn't believe him. Not if I say I didn't. Besides, he knows better than to cross me. Don't you, Robbie?"

Robbie shrugged, but he didn't say anything. He was obviously afraid of Angel. She had him in her power.

"Robbie, do you want to come upstairs and play?" Amanda asked.

Angel hunched her shoulders and stepped toward Amanda as if she might charge. "He can't. This is my house, and I won't let him."

Robbie shook his head in silent warning at Amanda who turned to leave.

"That's the way out," Angel said, pointing to a door

50

that could only be unlocked from inside the garden. She folded her arms defiantly.

Amanda let herself out.

* * *

"Have you made friends with the children downstairs yet, Amanda?" Mother asked during their supper of barbecued chicken and canned peas.

"Angel's not very nice, Mother."

"Well, but darling, if she's the only girl around—"

"I like Robbie. He's only ten, but he's smart. Angel's mean to him."

"Umm," Mother said. "Well, you keep out of it. That's not your business." The phone rang and Mother jumped up to answer it.

"Tony!" she chimed. "No, of course I'm not mad at you. . . . Why, I'd love to go out for a drink. No, she won't mind staying alone. Will you, Amanda?" Mother asked over her shoulder.

Amanda shook her head. She did mind staying alone in this unfriendly place, but not enough to ask Mother to stay home to keep her company. Giving up her pleasure for her daughter's sake was more than Amanda expected of her mother.

Amanda washed their supper dishes while Mother got dressed.

"Next time," Mother said, "Tony and I'll do something where you can join us."

"You said he doesn't like children."

Mother looked uncomfortable. "I can't help that, Amanda." Then she excused herself. "You know, I work awfully hard in a job that doesn't use half my capability just to make a living for us, and I need *some* recreation. . . . With other adults, I mean. You understand that, don't you, darling?"

Amanda nodded.

"This weekend I'll take you anywhere you want to go, just the two of us, okay?"

"Yes, Mother."

"I don't want you to be sorry you came. I know you were happy with Pearly."

"I'm glad to be with you."

"Good, because I love having you here when I get home from work. You're my pal, Amanda."

The statement pleased Amanda. In return, she offered, "You look beautiful."

"Not too old and ugly yet?"

"No."

Mother's sapphire eyes lit in a smile and she did look beautiful.

At the knock on the door, Amanda headed for her bedroom, but Mother called to her from the doorway where she stood facing a man. "Amanda, I want you to meet my friend, Tony Horton."

"Hi," Amanda said. Her hand was on her doorknob, but as it turned out, she didn't have to hide herself away.

"Hi, kid." Tony Horton waved at her without crossing the threshold. He looked ordinary, younger than Mother, but ordinary as if he might chew gum and leave his undershirt showing at the neck of his shirt, things Mother had cautioned Dale against more than once. A minute later the door closed behind them and Mother was gone.

Amanda was reading when she heard Robbie's one-three-two rhythm knock on the door and his voice saying, "It's me."

She let him in.

"Here," he said, handing her a small brass key. "Hide it good for me, please."

"Too bad about your drawing pad."

"Yeah, it cost a couple of allowances. I'll have to save up for another one. And wouldn't you know, last week my mother forgot to send me my allowance." Anxiously he added, "Usually she writes once a week, but she didn't send a letter either. Unless something's wrong with her."

"Probably not, Robbie."

"Maybe she's just busy," he said. "She doesn't get to sleep much in the hospital. They make interns do all the work. She's strong though, and I promised her I would be, too. But how'd I know about Angel? I mean, Mom said Moira was so nice, but she sure didn't get a nice kid."

"Does Angel know you came up here?"

"No, but she'll figure it out. There's not that many places I can be. Don't let her in if she comes to the door."

"I'm never letting that girl in my house," Amanda said.

Robbie sighed. "So what do you want to play?"

"I want to show you something first." The time for the test had come. Amanda felt solemn. She brought Pink Pig to Robbie and said, "Here. Put out your hand."

Trustingly, Robbie thrust his hand out. Amanda set

53

Pink Pig down on his palm. Pink Pig was no bigger than an almond, but her curly tail stuck out proudly and her translucent ears were large and important. Her tiny black eyes studied Robbie intently.

Robbie stood still for a long minute. Then he whispered, "It's magic, isn't it?"

"How do you know?" Amanda asked.

"Because I feel it."

Amanda took a deep breath. "This is my friend, Pink Pig," she said.

All at once, Pink Pig began to grow. In an inkling, the three of them were standing on a country road in the Little World under a bright blue sky.

five

"There's the castle, Robbie." Amanda pointed to the high, stone, turreted walls on a hill beyond the sunny fields. "You can really see it now that Wizard's gone. He used to make clouds to hide it."

"You should have seen when the dark knight tried to work Wizard's magic." Pink Pig oinked in amusement. "He came up with rainbows instead of clouds."

"Rainbows would be nice," Amanda said. "Rainbows would be beautiful." The Little World looked wonderful to her, after not having seen it in six months.

Robbie was hopping about, too excited to stand still. "Boy, that's a neat castle! Boy, would I love to explore that place."

"But you can't," Pink Pig warned him. "Or you'll end up in the castle dungeon. . . . We'd better go ask Frog what the dark knight's up to before we do anything here."

"Who's Frog?" Robbie asked.

55

"Frog knows everything and he's sort of funny," Amanda said. "He lives back there in a pond in a woods." She pointed behind her, past the fields where the woods began.

"Funny?" Pink Pig sounded insulted on her friend's behalf. "Frog's not funny. He's a serious fellow."

"But he talks in rhyme," Amanda said.

"Oh, well, if that's your idea of funny."

Suddenly Amanda noticed that Robbie was staring openmouthed at something in the field. Then she saw it, a pair that did seem strange even for the Little World. Spangled Giraffe, sequins aglitter, was high-stepping along the border of the field, pulling a plow behind his long, lanky body. Holding the handles of the wooden plow was Ballerina. Her pink tutu bobbed as she minced along the furrow.

"Whatever is going on!" Amanda exclaimed.

"I told you things weren't good in the Little World," Pink Pig said.

"But Ballerina's a dancer, not a farmer," Amanda said. Without another word, they all three went dashing toward her through the daisies and buttercups of the unworked part of the field.

"Why are you plowing?" Amanda asked Ballerina breathlessly.

Ballerina's dainty hand went to her throat in amazement at the sight of Amanda. Then she threw her arms around Amanda and kissed her on both cheeks, but her joy at seeing Amanda back in the Little World was short lived. Almost at once, Ballerina began peering about as if they might be watched. She nodded toward the castle and secretively showed Amanda her delicate white hands. They were pitifully blistered and sore.

"Can't she talk?" Robbie whispered to Amanda.

"Not everyone in the Little World talks," Amanda explained as she tried to console Ballerina with a hug. "Some you think should be able to can't, like Ballerina and Peasant Man and Peasant Woman, but Frog and Pink Pig can talk very well."

"What Ballerina's trying to tell us," Pink Pig said to Robbie, "is that Dark Knight makes her plow. It's plow or get thrown in the dungeon without food or water. He wants everyone to be useful. You work or provide food for him someway."

"But dancing's useful. It's entertaining," Amanda said.

"Dark Knight doesn't think so," Pink Pig said.

Sadly Ballerina picked up her plow handles. She and Spangled Giraffe, who'd taken advantage of the stop to take a treetop snacking break on some tender leaves, got back to work. Birds still sang with total confidence in the calm sky above the empty field, but the Little World no longer seemed to be as happy a place as it had been when Amanda last saw it.

"It's just as bad as in the real world," she complained.

"Except you can change things here," Pink Pig said.

"How?"

"You got rid of Wizard. Now the dark knight's in power."

"You mean fight the dark knight," Amanda said.

57

"But how? We're not strong, and we don't even have any weapons."

"I have heard that another knight is coming to lay claim to Wizard's castle," Pink Pig said. "Suppose he's a good knight, and suppose we help him, and suppose he wins—"

"That's a lot of supposes," Amanda said.

"But, Amanda, we can try," Robbie put in eagerly. "I always wanted to be a knight and fight battles and stuff like that." He put up his fist to flex his muscle. It barely bulged. "Well, I'll help him if I can. If he wants me to. Somehow," Robbie said doubtfully.

"We were going to talk to Frog," Amanda reminded them.

They continued on into the woods through pockets of shadows and shafts of sunlight. "This is fun," Robbie said as they crossed a mossy brook. "This is the most fun I've had since my parents stuck me with Angel. Thanks for letting me come along, Pink Pig."

"You may be sorry you came," Pink Pig said. "Trouble in the Little World can be dangerous."

That reminded Amanda of the time when Pink Pig was Wizard's prisoner. "But what about you, Pink Pig?" Amanda said. "What does this dark knight want of you?"

"Last time he saw me snoozing in the sun, he said I'd be the main dish at his victory dinner when he stops fighting," Pink Pig said.

"Pink Pig!" Amanda cried. "What are you doing about that?"

"Keeping out of sight as much as I can. Don't worry,

58

Amanda. Dark Knight likes fighting too much to stop for a feast."

Amanda hoped that was true.

"Why's it called the Little World?" Robbie asked. "Everything looks normal size to me."

"That's because you're in proportion to the folk that live here. In Amanda's world, I can grow a little, but here she gets small and so did you."

"Really? Wow. You mean Angel could stick me in her pocket now?"

"If she could see you."

"I'd hate to be small enough for Angel to squash. But if she can't see me, maybe I could just hang out here until my parents come to get me. Angel's gotta be more dangerous than anything here."

"Don't let the sunshine and blue sky fool you," Pink Pig said and stopped moving because they had arrived at the edge of Frog's pond.

"Who's that?" Amanda asked.

A brown man with a beard, wearing brown leather armor, was sitting on the bank with his bare feet in the water. Seeing them, he called out in a voice like a bassoon, "Hot day, isn't it? Don't be shy. Come right on over here and cool your feet in this pool with me."

"Who are you?" Amanda asked.

"You first. Who are *you?*" he demanded, bugging his eyes at her in a humorous way.

Amanda introduced herself, and then Robbie and Pink Pig. "We're visitors here," she said, "all except Pink Pig."

"Well, welcome folks. Pleased to meet you. I'm

known as the brown knight. If you're as peaceable as you look, you can be my guests at the castle soon as I've claimed it."

"Doesn't the castle belong to the dark knight?" Pink Pig asked.

"Temporarily, only temporarily." The brown knight's grin was broad. "See, that sly old wizard promised it'd be mine after he died, which event I've only just discovered. That's why I'm here, to collect on his promise." The brown knight drew one muscular leg from the water and probed at a blister on his big toe.

Except for his muscles and his short black beard, he didn't look very fierce to Amanda. He had an open, friendly face, and his eyes were melted chocolate. A deep gravelly voice from the pond interrupted Amanda's inspection.

"I've given Brown Knight the word. All there is to know, he's heard. Let's hope that he can fight our terrible Dark Knight."

"Frog!" Robbie said. "I heard you talked in rhyme. Where are you?"

"As you hear, I'm quite near," Frog said. He hopped over a rock and landed on a log in plain sight near the edge of the pond.

"Frog, you look so big and fat," Amanda said approvingly. Then realizing he might not feel complimented, she amended her remark. "I mean, so healthy." The last time she'd seen Frog, he'd been starving from the drought Wizard had caused in the Little World.

"Looks don't always tell. I don't feel so well."

"You don't? How come?"

"To keep Dark Knight from eating me, I must hide since I can't flee."

"Eat you?" Amanda asked. "Why would he do that?"

"As a worker, I don't rate. I'd serve better on his plate."

"He sounds as bad as Wizard," Amanda said.

"That Wizard!" Brown Knight said. "The day I set out to become a knight, I went adventuring in a Witches' wood and stumbled on him being cooked alive in a copper pot. He swore if I saved him, he'd leave me his castle and find me a wife to boot. Well, I'm a bachelor still, and as for the castle, Frog's just now told me how to find it. Good thing I'm an easygoing fellow or I'd be riled."

"Are you going to fight Dark Knight?" Robbie asked eagerly.

"Only if I have to, sonny."

"Well, do you need a squire to help you?"

"A squire?"

"You know, to help you carry your sword and stuff."

"I don't know as I'm that advanced in the knighthood business, but let's feel your muscle and see how you'd measure up to the job," Brown Knight said.

Reluctantly, Robbie surrendered his arm for examination. The brown knight stood up for the task. Standing, he looked enormous. His massive head and shoulders loomed over Robbie's slight figure. In silence he contemplated the skinny forearm. Then he retrieved his sword from behind a tree and offered it. Robbie grasped the heavy sword and would have staggered backward into the pond with it if Brown Knight hadn't steadied him.

"I think it's a mite big for you, sonny," Brown Knight said kindly.

Robbie mouth's turned down. Brown Knight laid a big hand on his shoulder and said, "How about you be my companion-in-waiting instead of a squire? Then instead of lugging stuff, you could just keep me company. I like company."

"Sure," Robbie said. "Fine. When do we leave?"

It amazed Amanda that Robbie sounded so brave here in the Little World when he'd acted so rabbity in Angel's garden. But then, Amanda had turned brave in the Little World, too, hadn't she? It must be something in the air, she decided as she asked Brown Knight, "Can we come, too? Pink Pig knows a lot about the Little World, and I can help her scout for you."

"Looks like I've got myself a regular army," the brown knight said with a night-lighting grin.

"You'll find them, I predict, the best you could've picked," Frog said.

CLICK. Amanda heard the key turning in the lock. "We have to go, Pink Pig," she said in alarm, and to Robbie, "My mother's back. We have to go."

"At once," Pink Pig said.

In an instant they were standing in Amanda's bedroom, and Pink Pig was miniature size again.

"It must be very late. Is your mother going to be mad I'm here?" Robbie whispered. "Do you want me to hide, Amanda?"

"I don't think she'll be mad, so long as I'm where I'm supposed to be," Amanda said.

62

She grabbed the first game that came to hand in her closet, Parcheesi. Together, she and Robbie set it up on the floor, and by the time Mother came to the door of Amanda's bedroom, they were playing.

"Amanda! I thought you'd be asleep. Do you realize how late it is?"

"Robbie came up to keep me company, and I guess we didn't look at the time," Amanda said. "That's all right, isn't it?"

"Yes, of course. How nice that you two made friends." Mother gave Robbie an approving smile. "But I think you'd better say goodnight and continue your game tomorrow."

"Sure," Robbie said. "Nice to meet you, Mrs. Bickett."

"Come back soon. If you get scolded for being out so late, you may tell Mrs. Delaney to call and speak to me about it," Mother offered.

"I'll tiptoe. They won't even know I was gone. Usually I go to my room right after dinner to get away from Angel. They don't care what I do. They watch TV all night."

Mother frowned. "I'm sure Mrs. Delaney cares what you do, Robbie. And why should you have to get away from Angel? . . . Never mind," she put in as Robbie opened his mouth to answer her. "You can tell me some other time."

Amanda walked Robbie to the door and saw why Mother was in a hurry. Tony Horton was sitting on the living room couch with his arm stretched along the back, looking very comfortable. Amanda said goodnight to Robbie, then smiled at Tony Horton.

"Hi, kid," he said. "You're up kind of late, aren't you?"

"I'm going to bed now," she assured him.

He nodded and looked away as if he didn't have anything else to say to her.

Mother was in the kitchen dropping ice cubes on the floor. "Can I help you?" Amanda turned to ask.

"No, darling. You just go on to bed. Tony and I will manage fine by ourselves."

"Goodnight then," Amanda said to Tony.

He flicked a finger at her as if she were an ash he was getting rid of.

She decided against taking a shower before she went to bed. The sooner the light was out in her room, the happier Mother would be. Quickly, Amanda brushed her teeth, used the toilet, and got in bed. She had a lot to think about. Things were going to happen now that she'd gotten back into the Little World, exciting things. Somehow, they'd help Brown Knight get rid of the dark knight so that Ballerina wouldn't have to plow fields and Frog wouldn't get eaten. And what about Pink Pig? She was in danger of being eaten someday, too. Amanda shivered at that unbearable thought.

She heard her mother's light laugh, the party laugh that Mother brought out for social occasions or sometimes for Dale. Mostly Mother didn't laugh when it was just Amanda and her. A sudden downpour of loneliness drenched Amanda.

She wished Dale were here now. He'd know how to handle Angel. He'd say, "Don't let it bother you, kid," if Amanda told him how Megan didn't seem interested in sleeping over or doing anything Amanda suggested they could do after school. Megan just wanted to be lunch friends. Amanda sighed. "I don't much like it in L.A. so far," she'd tell Dale, and he'd understand. Mother didn't seem to understand things, but Dale could—if he had the time to listen. Maybe this weekend when he called Mother, Amanda could talk to him alone for a few minutes.

Tomorrow she'd write to him, a long letter, and another letter to Pearly. And tomorrow, she and Pink Pig and Robbie might go back to the Little World in the afternoon, after school—if Robbie could get away from Angel.

six

Not one, but two letters were in the mail for Amanda when she got home from school, one from Pearly and one from Dale. Dale's was the rarer treat so Amanda saved it for last.

"The weather here is rainy and cold for May," Pearly wrote. "My tulips never showed. Squirrels must've got them, but the lilacs came out nice. Flopsy got out on the road yesterday, and I nearly had a heart attack thinking how you'd feel if she got hit. Lucky I caught her in time. We miss you, me and the rabbits and the cats. Glad you made a friend in school. I expected you would, and I bet you're doing good in school even though you don't say. It makes me proud to have such a smart, sweet granddaughter, and I hope you like L.A. better soon. Your loving grandma, Pearly."

Amanda wondered if she should confide in Pearly how Megan talked everybody down all the time. The teacher was stupid. The other kids were snobs. Megan didn't seem to like anybody. But Pearly didn't believe in talking ill of people. Better not to complain about Megan to her, especially not in a letter. Besides, Pearly would just say that Amanda didn't need to be friends with a girl like that. But Megan was the only other girl in the class who wasn't paired up already. Nobody else had even offered a friendly smile and said hi to Amanda.

Dale's letter went on for four pages. ". . . Sorry I only had time to kiss you hello at the airport, Little Mouse, but my hot and heavy romance was taking all my free time. It's over now. We fought too much. Frankly, it's got me down. Mom should be glad. She never was too enthused about Louanne. Well, you know Mom. Even though I went off and joined the army instead of being smart enough to go to Harvard like she wanted, she still doesn't think any girl's good enough for me.

"My next leave should be about when your school lets out, and we'll go to Disneyland. Don't let Mom take you. I want to be the first. We can whoop it up on the rides, and I'll buy you a big Mickey Mouse—or did you get too grown up for that stuff? I can't believe how long it's been since we did anything together, but we'll fix that. Miss you. Luv you, Dale."

Amanda sighed with pleasure and reread the letter slowly before tucking it into the decorated folder where she kept all her mail.

She was still smiling when she went to see what was going on in the garden. Angel was out there screaming at her mother who was weeding with her basket beside her. "Well, where is he?" Angel yelled as if her mother, who was kneeling on the grass next to her, couldn't hear. "You must know where he is. He wouldn't just leave without telling you where he was going. Not my daddy."

Moira looked up at Angel with a sad, solemn face. "But he did, Angel," she said. "I'm sorry, but he did."

"How come then? What'd you do? You must've done something to him. You must've made him mad."

"You know how hard I've tried to please your father." Moira bent back to her weeding.

"You're so stupid," Angel said. "My daddy might not like you anymore, but he likes me. You're just trying to keep him away from me, but you can't. I'll run away and I'll find him."

"Angel," Moira stopped pulling weeds and looked up. "I know you love your father. I'm sorry he's gone, and if I knew where, I'd tell you, believe me. If I even knew *why* he left—I suspect he just got bored with us. We don't provide enough excitement for him."

"Bored with you, you mean. You don't do anything but dig in the dirt. You're just a big fat blob." Angel burst into tears and ran into the house. Moira sat there with her head hanging and her shovel still. Her shoulders began to shake with sobs, and Amanda swallowed, hurting for Mrs. Delaney whose husband was gone and whose only child was a brat.

Amanda picked up her book to comfort herself. She got so lost in it that she didn't hear Robbie's knock until he called, "Amanda, are you there? It's me."

As soon as she let him in, she told him what she'd seen in the garden. "Why's Angel so mean to her mother?"

"I don't know. Because Moira lets her be, I guess. I think something's wrong with Moira. She used to smile

68

a lot when I first came, and she talked to me and asked me what I was doing in school. She likes my mother. She said my mother's a super lady, and she talked about how she was going to get a career like my mom because writing poetry didn't matter to anyone. But now Moira sits around all day and she doesn't even smile. It's too bad if her husband left."

"My father left," Amanda said. "My mother's still mad at him for it, even though he's been dead a long time. I don't know why fathers do that to their families."

"Well, they don't all. My dad takes good care of us. And he's easygoing, like the brown knight sort of. And he writes me funny letters. But I wish he didn't take that grant. He just took it so they'd give him tenure at the university maybe." Tears filmed Robbie's eyes, and he swiped them with his hand.

"When will he be back for you?" Amanda asked.

"Two more months. He gave me a calendar to check off the days. They sure pass slow. I hate it here, Amanda."

"Me, too," she whispered.

"Well, you've got your mother."

Amanda shook her head.

"Why not?"

Amanda didn't want to talk about it. She just knew she felt more lonely here in Los Angeles than she'd ever been in her life. In Schenectady, before Mother had lost her job, Amanda had been alone a lot, but she'd had friends there, and Dale sometimes, when he wasn't out doing sports or hacking around with his buddies. Here, after Robbie left, Pink Pig was the only one to count on. Even though Mother said she liked having Amanda around and that they were pals, Amanda knew Mother would rather be with Tony or somebody who wasn't a child. Like Tony, Mother didn't seem to find children very interesting, and Amanda had a lot of years to go before she turned into an adult.

"Do you think Pink Pig would get me into the Little World again, Amanda?" Robbie said. "I'd like to see how Brown Knight's doing."

"You're the only one she's ever taken in besides me. She must like you," Amanda assured him, and Robbie smiled proudly.

Pink Pig oinked with relief when they greeted her. "We better hurry," she said. "They're having their first battle, and the dark knight's got his dragon with him."

They arrived in the Little World at the end of the field where the forest began in time to see Brown Knight racing toward the woods just ahead of the dragon's flaming breath.

"Yeow!" Brown Knight yelled as the dragon got the back of his neck. He reached a thicket, dove in head-first and began crawling rapidly to the middle beyond the dragon's reach.

"He's running away." Robbie sounded disappointed.

"Wouldn't you run away from a dragon?" Amanda asked.

"But I thought he'd be brave."

"He may be," Pink Pig said. "If he tries to win another way, he may be brave and smart. That's better than brave and dead."

Something made Amanda turn. A chill snaked through her as she saw the dark knight standing on a hill behind them encased in armor from head to toe. With his face invisible behind his steely helmet, he didn't even look human. Most scary of all was that he seemed to be looking their way.

"Duck, Pink Pig. Get out of sight," Amanda warned, and Pink Pig scooted behind a bush.

The dragon was prowling back and forth at the edge of the thicket. Every so often it breathed out a blow torch that shriveled leaves and made the bushes seem to shrink back. Brown Knight had disappeared from view.

"Let's get out of here," Amanda said.

At that very instant the dark knight raised his mailed fist and pointed their way. The dragon reared, changed direction, and charged at them. Pink Pig's legs were short. She squealed in terror as she fell behind on their dash into the woods. Amanda stopped and scooped her up.

Robbie was climbing a tree. The dragon crashed through a pair of saplings and landed at the base of it.

"Yikes, he's going to get me," Robbie yelled.

"Brown Knight, help us!" Amanda screamed.

Brown Knight came jogging through the trees carrying a sloshing wooden bucket full of water. Flames shot from the dragon's mouth, burning the tree where Robbie clung. With a mighty heave, Brown Knight doused the flames with his bucket of water. The dragon grunted in surprise and looked around as if to say, "What do I do about that?" Close to it now, Amanda saw how wrinkled its neck was. The green scales had worn off in patches near its hips, and its eyes were bleary. The dragon's old, Amanda thought.

71

She put her finger to her lips to warn Robbie and Pink Pig to be quiet. Everyone but the dragon stood still, barely breathing. It snuffled around, grunting to itself, as if it were trying to smell them out. Finally, it gave up and lumbered out of the woods.

"Whew," Brown Knight said. "Good thing I found that bucket on the bank of the stream back there or you'd have been a goner, sonny."

"You saved my life," Robbie said. He shimmied down the tree.

"Just doing my job," Brown Knight said with a grin.

"And you saved me," Pink Pig murmured to Amanda who stroked her rubbery head with love.

"Well, good buddies," said Brown Knight as he gingerly touched the back of his neck. "Looks like we better put our heads together and come up with a battle plan. We'll need a good one to defeat an enemy with a dragon on his side. Meanwhile, I'll make a poultice for my burns."

"A poultice?" Pink Pig asked.

"Some medicinal herbs in a little wet mud to ease the sting."

"Are you a doctor?"

"Well, I've been known to do some healing now and then."

"We could use a doctor in the Little World," Pink Pig said.

"What for?" Robbie asked.

"For Peasant Man and Peasant Woman's arthritis," Amanda guessed. "They're old and achy."

"And Ballerina takes a bad fall sometimes," Pink Pig said.

"I know what," Robbie said to Brown Knight suddenly. "We can tie the dragon up when its sleeping, and then you can fight the dark knight, can't you?"

"What are we going to tie him up with? String?" Brown Knight asked. "Good try, sonny, but we've gotta do better." He patted Robbie on the shoulder encouragingly.

"We could dig a big pit and trap him in it," Robbie suggested.

"Umm," Brown Knight said. "Now that's an idea."

"But if we dig a pit near the castle—it has to be where the dragon goes around the castle, doesn't it?—" Amanda said, "then the dark knight'll see us."

"We could dig at night," Robbie offered.

"Maybe we could tame the dragon," Amanda said. "I once read a story about a boy who tamed a wolf by feeding it. Maybe we could feed the dragon and it would get to like us."

Brown Knight stroked his pointy beard. "Umm, sounds peaceful. I like peaceful ways to win." He winced.

"Does your burn hurt a lot?" Amanda asked sympathetically.

"It could feel better. I'll take a poultice-making break now."

"Did the wizard teach you about herbs?" Pink Pig asked.

"No, my daddy did. He was a doctor. I would've been one, too, if I hadn't wanted to try this knight business."

"You could be a doctor here after you defeat the dark knight," Amanda said.

73

"I could maybe, after I get tired of lolling around on the throne. . . . Say, who's this ballerina you keep mentioning?"

"She danced for us," Pink Pig said. "But Dark Knight has her pulling a plow now."

"Poor lady!" Brown Knight said. "Looks like we'd better dump this dark knight fast. Let's try Amanda's idea of how to do it."

As he'd been talking, he had been collecting small plants. Now he began mashing them into a paste on a stone. Robbie brought him mud from the stream. Brown Knight lay down on his stomach with his head on his arms and Robbie laid on the poultice.

"So what are we going to feed the dragon to tame it?" Robbie asked.

"Anything," Pink Pig said. "That dragon's always hungry. It even eats whatever it can from the castle's garbage. Then it has to burn up whatever it can't eat. It really works two jobs—guard and garbage."

"You don't say!" Brown Knight said. "Well, that ought to make it pretty easy to convince the big old lizard it'd get better treatment from us. What's its favorite food?"

"I don't know," Pink Pig said. "We could ask Ballerina. She knows what goes on in the castle." Without further ado, they all set off.

Ballerina was there in the field, wearing her tutu and steering the plow behind Spangled Giraffe. Her body was bow shaped from weariness, and Spangled Giraffe's neck drooped in a second weary bow.

Brown Knight took one look at Ballerina, and his expressive face glazed over. "Wow!" he said and socked

74

his chest. "I'm smitten." He strode ahead and fell on one knee beside the plow to ask, "If I save you from the dark knight, will you marry me, beautiful lady?"

Ballerina halted and looked wonderingly at the stranger.

"This is Brown Knight," Amanda told her. "He's here to claim the castle. Wizard promised it to him."

Ballerina clapped her small white hands with delight, but then she shook her head, her finger, too, in Brown Knight's face for emphasis. And to explain her double negative, she dropped the plow, twirled on one foot, then made a beautiful leap to the next furrow, ending with a *révérence*.

"I think she's trying to tell you that she's dedicated to her art," Pink Pig said. "She can't get married."

"Is that right?" Brown Knight asked.

Ballerina nodded proudly.

"Can't she talk?" Brown Knight whispered.

"No," Amanda said. "Some people here can't."

"No kidding," Brown Knight said. He shook his head in pity. Then he turned to Ballerina and said, "Well, drop that plow and start dancing, honey. I'm going to take care of you, and you can be my lady whether you marry me or not. I'll even do the cooking."

Ballerina looked at him thoughtfully. She touched his cheek, but she shook her head, and with a fearful glance at the castle, she picked up the plow again.

"You mean you'd rather be a slave than take a chance on me?"

Ballerina shrugged expressively.

"She's afraid," Pink Pig said. "After all, if you lose—"

"But I won't," Brown Knight said. "Tell us Dragon's favorite food, and we'll go off, tame him, take over the castle, and be back in a jiffy."

Ballerina smiled. She took Brown Knight's hand, pulled it down to a furrow, pretended to bury it, then pantomimed waiting. Finally, she dug up the hand, brushed the dirt off it, and pretended to eat it.

Charades, Amanda thought and guessed, "A vegetable. A root vegetable, like a potato maybe." To her, Brown Knight's lumpy fist looked a bit potatolike.

"That's it," Pink Pig said. Ballerina was nodding. She pointed toward the horizon where they could just see the chimney of a small cottage beyond the fields. "Peasant Man and Peasant Woman's hut," Pink Pig said. "What they grow mostly is potatoes."

"Let's go ask them for some then," Amanda said.

They set off immediately, leaving Ballerina to catch Spangled Giraffe who was snacking on tree tops again.

"Imagine making that beautiful lady plow fields!" Brown Knight said. "Maybe I ought to go punch Dark Knight out without taking time to fool around with his dragon." He suddenly brandished his sword and charged a bush in an excess of passion. "Take that you varlet, and that, and that." Chunks of quaking leaves fell left and right.

"I'm ready," Robbie said. "Let's go."

"Not yet," Pink Pig advised. "You'll both get killed."

"Let's stick to our plan for winning the dragon over," Amanda urged.

"Meanwhile Ballerina's hurting," Brown Knight said.

"She didn't even say she'd marry you," Amanda said.

76

"Don't worry. Once I'm a hero, she'll marry me. That's how it always happens."

"In stories," Amanda said.

"Or on TV," Robbie put in.

"I think we should talk to the peasant folk," Pink Pig insisted.

"You are supposed to collect information on the enemy before going into battle," Robbie said. "Anyway, that's what generals do in the war books I read."

"All right, all right, all right," Brown Knight agreed in his deep, musical voice. "We'll go see the farmers, but if they won't help us, it's straight to the castle for me."

It was a long walk to the cottage. Before they'd arrived, the phone rang in the real world, and Amanda had to leave the Little World to go and answer it.

"Amanda, is Robbie up there?"

"Yes, Mrs. Delaney. Do you want him?"

"Well, the one I'm really looking for is Angel. Is she with you?"

"No." Amanda tried to remember. "I didn't see her on the bus either."

"She didn't say anything to you about going somewhere after school?"

Amanda heard the anxiety in Moira's voice and didn't want to make it worse by saying she and Angel didn't talk at all. "I don't know where she is," Amanda said simply.

"If she had a friend, perhaps—" Moira said, and then she asked, "Let me speak to Robbie, please. He's in her class. He might know."

Amanda put her hand over the receiver, but she

didn't have to call for him. Pink Pig and Robbie were standing there beside her already. In silence, Amanda handed Robbie the phone.

"She doesn't have any friends in school," Robbie told Moira. Amanda carried Pink Pig to the living room window. Robbie joined them there when he finished talking.

"Moira thinks Angel must have gone looking for her father," Robbie said.

"But how would she get around? Everything's too far to walk around here," Amanda pointed out.

"I wouldn't put it past Angel to hitchhike," Robbie said.

"To where?"

Robbie shrugged. "To wherever she thinks her father is."

"Is Moira going to call the police?" Amanda asked.

"I guess if Angel's not back before dark, she will," Robbie said. "I wouldn't worry about Angel, though. She's tough."

* * *

That evening, Mother was doing her bills at the dinette table while she listened to chamber music. The full moon was lighting up the garden, and Amanda leaned against the window to admire the silvery effect. Near where she had seen Moira weeping by the red flowers, was another heaving back. This time it was Angel who was crying. She hadn't found her father, Amanda guessed, but at least she was back home. Good. Now Moira could stop worrying about her.

seven

Mother woke up in a good mood late that Saturday morning. "Today I'm taking you to the beach," she announced. "One advantage of L.A. is we're close to the ocean, not like in Schenectady. There we needed a whole week's vacation to make the drive worthwhile."

Amanda couldn't recall ever spending a week at a beach with Mother. It must have happened before she was five. She didn't remember much before getting Pink Pig on her fifth birthday. Pearly had sent the miniature as an anonymous gift because Mother hadn't been willing to let her in their lives back then.

"It'd be fun to go to the ocean," Amanda said. "I saw it from the plane, I think."

"Probably you did, yes. . . . We'll drive to Malibu. Oh, do you have a swimsuit?"

"Pearly bought me one for a pool party, but I didn't get to use it because that's when you said you got the apartment and I should come."

79

Mother raised an eyebrow. "Hmmm. Well, I'm sure there'll be plenty of pool parties to go to here."

Amanda wasn't so sure. Megan had said she had a swimming pool, but she'd added quickly, "I can't invite people to use it, though," as if she were afraid Amanda might demand an invitation. Every day Megan ate lunch with her and teamed up with her automatically when they had to work in pairs, and yet they weren't friends. Mother had said Amanda was welcome to invite a friend to sleep over, but when Amanda had invited Megan, she'd said she couldn't. Then she'd added meanly, "Anyways, your apartment sounds like a prison if you can't even go for a walk." What Amanda wondered was why Megan hung around with her since she didn't seem to like Amanda much. Unless it was because, like Amanda, Megan didn't have anyone else to be with.

While Mother packed a picnic lunch, Amanda made her bed and got into her bathing suit. It was a little baggy. Pearly had bought it without her at a pre-season sale the day after Amanda got the pool party invitation.

"You're really too thin for a tank suit," Mother said when she saw Amanda in it. "And pink! Trust Pearly to pick pink. It's not your color, Amanda. Aqua would suit you better or maybe a coral."

Amanda squirmed self-consciously.

"Never mind," Mother said. "Next time we go shopping, I'll get you something more becoming."

Mother was tall and slim, and Dale was very tall, over six foot. Only Amanda was small. She didn't look like her father either according to Pearly. His grin was what showed best in the picture Pearly had of him. Everything Amanda knew about her father, Pearly had told her. Mother had never talked about him because he'd deserted her after Amanda was born. From what Pearly said, her father had been an easygoing, good-hearted man. Amanda thought she would have liked him.

"Anyway, it's very comfortable." Amanda spoke up in Pearly's defense, remembering how her grandmother's cheerful, lumpy face had lit up when that invitation came, as if it were for her. Pearly, Amanda thought with a sudden longing like a cramp in her stomach.

Mother wore a floating cotton jacket over her swimsuit and carried a big straw hat. Both were new, and so were the rolled up bamboo mats Mother handed Amanda to carry. "Do you go to the beach a lot, Mother?"

"I haven't been since my first date with Tony." Wistfully, Mother added, "When he asked me, I rushed out and bought a suit and beach bag and these mats thinking we'd go often. . . . I'm not twenty years old anymore, but my figure's still good. I don't know why he's never taken me again."

The phone rang and Mother answered. Amanda stood holding the beach mats, waiting to leave. "Tony!" Mother sang out. "Tony, you just caught me. My daughter and I are on our way to Malibu. Yes, it certainly is a beautiful day. Why don't you join us? . . . I see. Well, of course . . . This evening? I think I'm free. Just let me check the calendar."

Amanda looked at the calendar which was blank except for the dental appointment Mother had made for her to have a check-up.

"All right, tonight at seven then." Mother hung up smiling and let her breath out. "Well, well, well! Let's go, sweetie. I want to get back early so I can do my nails and hair."

In the car, Mother chatted about her job. "This woman I work for is moody. Some days she's my pal and tells me her troubles and other days she's rude and issues orders as if— What bothers me most is I could do her job better than she does, but there's no way I'll ever get a chance at it. She's not married, and she's gotten as high as she's likely to get in the organization. She'll hang on 'till she dies. I'm blocked forever if I stay there."

"Are you going to look for another job?"

"I might. I should . . . eventually."

Amanda wondered if Mother would send her back to Pearly if she changed jobs. That would be good. Or maybe Mother would find a different apartment at least. Amanda reminded herself of another good possibility in her life. "Dale said he's coming to visit us soon, Mother."

"Yes. Thank heavens. The last time we spent a weekend together was in February."

"I haven't seen him since forever," Amanda said.

Mother smiled at her. "You always did adore your big brother, didn't you?"

"He's going to take me to Disneyland."

Mother laughed. "Dale's still boy enough to enjoy the place."

"Have you been to Disneyland?"

"I've been too busy," Mother said. "First it was finding a job, and taking that night course on computers. Then I had to locate our apartment, and furnishing it was a mammoth task. Besides, going places alone isn't much fun, and sunny California's not an easy place to make new friends."

"Why?"

"Who knows? People just don't seem to connect easily. Well—" Mother sighed. "At least, I don't have to avoid embarrassing questions."

Amanda wondered if Mother was embarrassed about her trouble with the bank, when she'd borrowed that money without asking because she'd wanted Dale to go to a fancy college. Dale hadn't even wanted to go. That had been a bad time in their lives. Mother had repaid the money and moved to California to start over, and Dale had joined the army. But Amanda was glad she'd chosen to stay behind with Pearly. The months with her had been fun.

"Never mind, darling," Mother said. "Tell me about your friends. Tell me about Angel and Robbie. Do you like them?"

"I like Robbie."

"Not Angel?"

"She's mean."

Mother waited to hear more. That was new, having Mother interested in what she thought. It perked Amanda up. But how much could she tell without running into misunderstandings? The time she'd told about the Little World, Mother had sent her to a psy-

83

chologist as if Amanda were crazy. "Do you know Angel didn't come home from school yesterday?"

"No," Mother said. "Where did she go?"

"To find her father maybe."

"And did she find him?"

"I don't know." Amanda thought of the sad figure in the garden last night. "Probably not. She got home all right, though."

"Angel's father's a crude sort of man from what I could see," Mother said. "His voice is so loud, and his clothes are sloppy. If he's left for good, I can't imagine Moira Delaney's lost much. She's a cultured person, a poet. She went to an elite college with Robbie's mother."

"But Angel wants her father." Amanda thought of the awful way Angel had spoken to her mother. "I think she likes her father best."

Mother gave her a sharp look. "Children can't be expected to know what's good for them. The parent who sacrifices the most for a child is often the least appreciated. Fathers!" Mother said bitterly. "The fathers who do nothing for them get preference over the mothers who stay around to do the work."

Amanda laid low in the silence that followed. She studied the jungly plants at the entrance to a shopping mall they were passing and wondered if the red tulips that she and Pearly had planted around the mailbox were blooming.

"I wouldn't have chosen that apartment if there hadn't been children you could play with there, Amanda. The house is so isolated. That pocket of neighborhood was left when they tore the rest down to build the freeway entrance. But I thought you'd be safe in the garden with Angel. It's really upsetting that you don't like her. Perhaps—"

"What's Malibu like?" Amanda interrupted desperately.

Ignoring the question, Mother went on. "Perhaps if you got to know Angel better."

"Robbie hides out in his room to keep out of her way."

"Oh, Amanda, really! Angel's just a little girl. Try being nice to her and she'll be nice back. Anyway, you like Robbie, don't you?"

"Yes . . . . Robbie wrote his father that he's worried about his mother. He thinks something might have happened to her because she hasn't called or written him. Robbie likes both his parents a lot."

"I'm sure his mother's just busy." Mother sounded normal again.

They were driving on a busy road now past fast-food restaurants and fancy restaurants with palm trees and a funeral home which was fanciest of all. Mother said, "Well, you asked about Malibu. You must have seen it on television. It's a place where surfers go, lots of young people. The beach is lovely, and when we've had enough sun, we'll leave and get in some window-shopping on the way home."

"I like the sun."

Mother wrinkled her nose. "Frankly, an hour of sticky sand and hot sun is quite enough for me. I prefer browsing in boutiques."

85

The sand, Amanda discovered, was delightful to wiggle into, warm and yielding. An enticing aroma of coconut oil from all the tanning lotion on the gleaming golden bodies around them vied with the scent of salt and seaweed. Amanda had fun running into the foamy white water up to her knees, only to dash back before a green breaker caught her. The water tugged like a live thing at her legs. The sun was hot and the water was chill and the contrast was delicious. She flung her wet body down on the bamboo mat next to Mother's. Mother was stretched out on her stomach, her white limbs carefully protected by sunscreen. Amanda had refused to use any, reminding Mother that she tanned instead of burning.

"Watch it," Mother murmured. "You'll get sand all over me."

When Mother fell asleep in the sun, Amanda was glad because she didn't want to leave the beach to go window-shopping. They had been there nearly two hours when Mother woke up.

"Amanda, I should have covered you with sunscreen, too. You're red!"

"No, I'm fine. I don't burn."

"Well, you did today. We'll put some Noxema on you when we get home."

Amanda nodded, although she didn't think anything that felt so good was going to hurt her. "Thank you for taking me to the beach, Mother. It was wonderful," she said.

Mother looked pleased. "I'm glad you've had fun, darling."

They strolled along a shopping street for a while, looking at the display windows of boutiques, at expensive clothing and jewelry that Mother couldn't afford to buy. People had always admired Mother's taste. "I wish you were rich," Amanda said.

"Why, darling?"

"Then you could have what you want."

Mother gave Amanda an appreciative glance and said, "Anyway, your sunburn becomes you." And when they were walking back to the car, she said, "You know, you may turn into a pretty girl, after all, Amanda."

The sharp edges to the compliment didn't bother Amanda. She was happy. It had been a lovely afternoon, the nicest she could remember spending with Mother.

While Mother was getting herself ready for her date with Tony Horton, Amanda stepped out on the balcony to see if Robbie was in the garden. He wasn't but Angel was. She was tossing a softball and chasing after it herself. It looked like a boring game. Amanda drew back to go get a book, but the movement caught Angel's eye.

"Hey, catch," she yelled and threw the soft ball high and hard toward Amanda's balcony. The ball dropped dangerously close to the sliding glass windows. "Toss it down to me," Angel ordered.

Amanda obliged.

"Come on down and let's play ball," Angel said.

"No, thank you."

"Why not?"

"I don't like playing catch."

"We could play something else."

"Where's Robbie?" Amanda asked.

"You mean your cute little boyfriend? He's in bed crying."

"What did you do to him?" Amanda demanded.

"Nothing. He found out his mother's sick in the hospital."

"That must be why he hasn't been hearing from her. Poor Robbie," Amanda said.

"He'll get over it. Come on down here, Amanda. Please!" Angel begged.

"I don't like the way you play."

Angel didn't ask what Amanda meant. "But I hate playing alone," she said. "I'll pay you if you come. I'll give you a dollar."

The idea of being paid to play with someone shocked Amanda. "You don't have to pay me. I'll come down if you want to play a board game."

"Chinese Checkers?"

"Okay. I don't care which one."

She went down the garage stairs and out and found Angel waiting at the garden door. Angel looked quite pleasant when she smiled.

"Why are you so mean to Robbie?" Amanda asked after they'd settled down on either side of an umbrella table with the game set up between them.

"He's just like my mother. She lets everybody walk all over her. I hate that. You've gotta be tough and hit back hard. That's what my father says."

Amanda wondered how tough Angel thought she was, pretty tough because Angel treated her well. She

88

didn't even seem to mind when Amanda won the Chinese Checkers game. "Want some soda or something?" Angel asked.

"Okay." Amanda thought if they went inside, she might get to see Robbie and have a chance to comfort him a little.

The living room was dark. The curtains were drawn, and furniture lined the white walls in shadowy squares and rectangles. "Where's your mother?" Amanda asked.

"She's having one of her days."

"Hmmm?"

"Some days she just stays in bed and sleeps. Today's one of her days. My mother used to be a poet, but she doesn't write anything anymore. I think she should go out and get a job like your mom."

Amanda looked toward the hall. The only open door was the one to the bathroom. The kitchen was brightly lit, though, and much bigger than the kitchen upstairs. "You didn't come home after school yesterday," Amanda said.

"I got the secretary to drive me to this place where my father goes. His friend works there. It's a bar. But they said they haven't seen him. I guess he's on a business trip or something. Sometimes he drives down to Mexico and he doesn't tell us."

"So how did you get home?"

Angel shrugged. "I got a ride, and then I called my mom to come get me."

"Who'd you play with before Robbie came?" Amanda asked while Angel poured her a glass of soda.

"Sometimes my daddy. He took me to the ballpark

once and to Disneyland. And I like TV. Sometimes I watch TV all day. You could come down and watch TV with me."

"Thanks, but most of the time I'd rather read," Amanda said.

"Not me. I hate reading. What do you and Robbie play? You two spent all that time together. You weren't reading, were you?"

"No, we were playing."

"What?"

"It's hard to explain." Amanda was being cautious.

"Oh, I know *that* kind of playing," Angel said nastily.

Amanda hastened to correct her. "We go places together, sort of like pretend games."

"Pretend games?"

"Yes."

Instead of pursuing the subject, Angel said, "I can have all the junk food I want. My daddy gives me a big allowance. Besides, I can make my mom buy whatever I want when we go to the supermarket. I like going to the supermarket. Do you?"

"I don't know," Amanda said. "My mother does the shopping on the way home from work."

"She's beautiful, your mother. She looks like an old movie star."

Amanda nodded.

"You're pretty, but you don't look like her."

"I'm not pretty," Amanda said.

"Prettier than me, anyway."

Amanda didn't know what to say. Angel wasn't

90

pretty. She was bulky and fierce looking. "You look good when you smile," Amanda said.

"I do?"

"Uh-huh, you've got a beautiful smile."

Angel glowed. "Gee, thanks," she said as if Amanda had told her something wonderful.

As soon as she'd finished her soda, Amanda said she had to go and get dinner started for her mother. Angel looked surprised. "Your mother's supposed to do that," she said. "All's I have to do is set the table and usually I don't. My mother can't make me do anything."

"What's so good about that?" Amanda asked.

Angel frowned and didn't answer her.

Funny, Amanda thought on her way upstairs, up close Angel wasn't so bad. Not much worse than Megan. Probably Angel was only really nasty when she thought she could get away with it, like with Robbie. It was sad about Robbie's mother. He had enough to feel bad about without his mother being sick, too.

eight

Amanda missed the school bus in the morning because the alarm didn't go off and she and Mother overslept. Mother drove her to school, fretting all the way about being late for work which made Amanda feel bad even though it wasn't her fault. She wondered how Robbie was doing and looked for him in the halls. Sometimes she glimpsed him in passing, but today she didn't see him.

On the bus going home, Angel sat hunched against the window, alone on the seat behind the driver. Because of their afternoon together, Amanda expected to hear Angel's loud voice demanding that Amanda sit with her, but Angel didn't even look up. Good, Amanda thought, and hurried down the aisle. Robbie was sitting alone in the back of the bus looking miserable.

"I heard about your mother," Amanda said as she slipped into the seat next to him. "What's the matter with her, Robbie?"

"She's in intensive care. She passed out. Something in her head they think, but they don't know yet." His voice was sad as a mourning dove's.

"That's awful. I'm really sorry."

"My dad called me when he got my letter. He said he hadn't wanted to tell me, at least until she was getting better, but she's not getting better. I told him I want to be there, but he says not yet. He's with her when the nurses'll let him be, and then he sleeps on somebody's couch, and there's no place for me." Robbie's cheek twitched and his lip trembled.

"I hope they find out what's wrong with her so they can fix it."

"Me, too. I flubbed a whole math test today. I just couldn't think."

She squeezed his hand and, to distract him from his own problem, said, "Angel looks as if she's in a bad mood."

"She got into trouble again. Angel was mouthing off. So the teacher made her sit with her back to us while we did math bingo. Good thing the teacher didn't hear her cursing. Angel just sat there cursing the whole period. She hates our teacher."

"Is she a good student?"

"Angel? Who knows? All she does is make trouble. She says school's stupid."

"Well, anyway, want to come up to my apartment, and we'll go see what the brown knight's up to?"

Robbie's face brightened at the suggestion. "Yeah."

But when they got off the bus and he started to follow Amanda into the garage, Angel barked at him, "You come with me, Robbie Morrison."

93

"Not now," he said.

"Now! You're not playing with her today; you're playing with me."

Robbie stood his ground. "I'll play with you later, Angel."

She folded her thick arms. "Remember how I made you eat dirt?" Robbie's lips drew down. He didn't answer but he seemed to shrink.

"You can't make him do anything," Amanda said.

Angel got a gleam in her eye. "Who says? Come on, Robbie." He wavered on the edge of giving in.

Quickly, Amanda suggested, "We could tell her mother."

Angel heard her and grinned. "Try it, why don't you?"

Amanda walked past her and rang the front doorbell. She could hear the television going, but no one came to the door. She pressed her finger on the button hard. Still no one came. Angel came dragging Robbie by one limp arm. Conquering him seemed to have cheered her up. She unlocked the door and told Amanda, "You can probably find my mama on the couch in the living room." Then she towed Robbie off to the kitchen.

"Mrs. Delaney?" Amanda called as she stepped into the living room.

Moira was indeed lying on the couch. She removed her eyes from the television set with great effort. She looked ill. "What do you want?" she asked Amanda.

"Please, Mrs. Delaney. Would you tell Angel she can't boss Robbie around? He doesn't want to play with her, but she said—"

Moira's head dropped back onto the couch pillow and

she moaned, "Oh, go away and leave me alone, will you? I've got too much on my mind to deal with child-ish problems today."

Amanda backed away at once in embarrassment. Moira's reaction dismayed her. Through the patio doors Amanda could see Angel and Robbie wrestling on the grass. Angel had Robbie down on his back. She was kneeling on his stomach and had his arms pinned. He looked as if he were in agony.

Amanda rushed outside. "Angel, what are you doing to him? Stop that." She tried to grab Angel's meaty arm, but was flung aside.

"All he has to do is say it," Angel said.

"Say what?"

"Say, 'I love you Princess Angel. You're so beau-tiful.'" Angel grinned evilly at Amanda, raised herself to a squat and plumped down on Robbie's gut again. The sound was so awful Amanda didn't know whether she was hearing her own scream or Robbie's.

"Say it, Robbie. Say it," she begged him.

He gasped out the words with his eyes closed. "Now let him go," Amanda said.

"No, he's got to kiss me first."

"You're disgusting, Angel," Amanda said.

Angel left Robbie lying on the ground whimpering as he tried to get back his breath. In a black fury, she spat out, "You! What makes you think you're something? You're nothing. You don't even *have* a father." She advanced on Amanda and swung at her with clenched fist, hitting her hard on the side of her face.

Amanda had never been hit before in her life. She

was too stunned to feel pain. She stood there not knowing what to do next.

Angel burst out laughing. "You going to run and tell my mommy again? Oh me, oh my. That scares me sooo much," she said in a high, pretend voice. Then she bent toward Amanda and said fiercely, "You better get out of here before I *kill* you."

Amanda backed off, but Robbie had risen to his knees and his flushed, tearful face made her bold. "Robbie, come on," Amanda said.

He looked at her wide-eyed for an instant. "He's not going anywhere until he kisses me," Angel said. She twisted Robbie's arm back and he yelped. When she let go, he curled into a helpless ball hiding his head against his knees. Angel kicked him.

Amanda gasped and ran into the house. Moira wasn't in the living room anymore, but Amanda no longer expected her to help anyway. She fled upstairs, found her mother's work number and dialed it. In a tumble of unfinished phrases, Amanda described Angel's behavior. Mother hesitated a long minute, but finally she said, "All right, I'll come right home."

As soon as she had put down the receiver, Amanda checked to make sure she had locked the door. She felt like a coward leaving Robbie down there in Angel's power, but what could she do? She wasn't any stronger than he was. Her throat was swollen and the side of her face burned. She went to look in the bathroom mirror and wet a facecloth with cold water to hold against her puffy, red cheek. Shuddering, she stood there as horrible images of what Angel could be doing to Robbie jangled in her head. She didn't go to the balcony to look. She didn't want to see, and anyway, if she were Robbie, she wouldn't want anyone watching her humiliation.

What she did do was write a letter telling Robbie's father that he had to come rescue his son from Angel. Even if Robbie's mother was dying, he had to come. Angel was horrible. "You have to get Robbie out of here," Amanda wrote. Later, she'd get the hospital's address.

When Amanda finally checked out the garden, it was empty. Her cheek throbbed and she had a headache. She was crying by the time Mother walked into the living room.

"Oh, Amanda. She hit you!" Mother took Amanda's face into her cool hands.

"I told you."

"But I didn't realize it was so hard. How dare she! That little bully. I'm going down to speak to her mother."

"It won't do any good. I tried to tell Mrs. Delaney about Robbie, but she wouldn't listen. She's sick, Mother."

"What do you mean 'sick'?"

Amanda described how she'd found Moira Delaney on the couch. "She must be feeling bad because Angel's father's gone."

"It sounds as if she's suffering from depression," Mother said. "I haven't really seen anything of her lately. If he's left, she could very well be depressed."

"I don't know, but she wouldn't help me."

Mother bit her lower lip. "You're making a case for us to leave here, aren't you? If Angel's so bad and

Moira's not in charge, this isn't the place for you to be alone. But Amanda, how am I going to find another apartment we can afford? You can't imagine how impossible it is . . . Unless—" She put her long polished nail against her lip. "I wonder if Tony would help. He has some contacts. . . . Meanwhile, you keep away from those people. Just come home and lock the door and don't have anything to do with any of them."

"What about Robbie?"

"Well, if you think it's okay to play with him—"

"No—I mean, Angel's torturing him, and his parents aren't around to protect him. She's stronger than he is, Mother. She beats him up and makes him do disgusting things. Like she made him eat dirt, and to-day—"

"I'll try to reach his father if you insist," Mother interrupted. "But we can't get more involved than that, Amanda. I can barely take care of us. I can't take on responsibility for another child."

"But you'll call his father?"

Mother hesitated. Reluctantly she promised, "If you get me the telephone number of the hospital. Not that it'll do much good. What can I say to him?"

"I'll tell him about Angel. You just get Robbie's father on the phone, Mother, and I'll tell him," Amanda said.

She wasn't surprised that Robbie didn't sneak out that evening and come upstairs to go into the Little World. He must be angry and hurting all over. Amanda hoped Angel hadn't done him any permanent damage.

The next morning she walked past Angel who seemed perfectly normal in the front seat of the school

98

bus. Robbie was in the back looking sick and sad. "Did she make you kiss her?"

He shrugged.

"My mother will call your father if you give me a phone number for the hospital, and I wrote a letter I can send him about you and Angel," Amanda said.

"No," Robbie shook his head. "Don't do that, Amanda."

"Why?"

"Because. You don't understand."

"What don't I understand?"

"I promised them I'd be brave and start taking care of myself. Like I used to go running to my mom every time some kid was mean to me. I got picked on a lot in school because . . . well, you know. And now that Mom's sick it's even more important." He looked at Amanda woefully. "Even my dad says I used to be a crybaby. He always tells people how I wouldn't go on the playground slides and swings when he took me when I was four."

"But Angel's bigger than you are."

He nodded. "She sure is. I don't think she'd kill me, though."

"But yesterday, what she did to you—"

He blushed furiously and said, "Don't tell anybody what she made me say. I'd rather kiss a toad than her."

Amanda wasn't sure what to think. Just not telling, just taking it without complaining was a kind of courage, but she admired him more in the Little World when he stood ready to fight back. It was dangerous for him not to let his father know he was suffering. "I wish I could help you with Angel," Amanda said.

"She could beat us both up. Forget it. I'm just going to hide out as much as I can."

Thinking about it didn't bring Amanda to any better solution than hiding out. She sighed and said, "What about going to the Little World?"

"Let's go tonight, okay?" It seemed to be an effort for him to talk to her. He kept looking out the window and not meeting her eyes.

"Okay," she said and let him be.

* * *

That night, Amanda had just finished her homework when she heard Robbie's tapping on the door. She let him in while Mother was on the phone churning out the charm for Tony Horton.

They walked past Mother to Amanda's bedroom. Pink Pig was waiting on the night table, and they whisked into the Little World without wasting time on greetings.

"What's been happening, Pink Pig?" Amanda asked.

"Not much. Brown Knight's spending all his time with Ballerina. He does her plowing in the morning, and in the afternoon they go swimming in the river. Good thing the dark knight's so busy fighting on his borders or they'd be in big trouble."

"Let's go find them," Robbie said. Amanda was glad to hear some enthusiasm in his voice.

The field buzzed with bees. Golden butterflies wafted from white to blue to yellow flower. Puff clouds decorated the sky, and even the gray castle walls looked soft and dreamy in the distance.

On the river bank they found Ballerina twirling on one leg while Brown Knight's hands on her waist held

100

her steady. They seemed to Amanda to be dancing to the music of the birds.

"I didn't know you were a dancer, too," she said to Brown Knight.

"Who me? I'm just giving the lady an assist. So how're you guys doing?"

"Okay," Robbie said. "Did you get the potatoes from Peasant Man and Peasant Woman?"

Brown Knight snapped his fingers. "Meant to. It slipped my mind. Say, pretty lady," his voice thrummed as he spoke to Ballerina, "you sure you got it right? Potatoes doesn't sound like proper dragon food."

Playfully she folded his fingers into a fist which she pretended to eat. Then she rubbed her stomach and smacked her lips with such droll gusto that Brown Knight laughed.

"Let's see if we can get a load of potatoes from Peasant Man and Peasant Woman," Amanda said.

"Let's," Brown Knight agreed. "Coming, Ballerina baby?"

Her eyes went to the castle. She shook her head in what looked like real fear and pointed at the field.

Brown Knight nodded. "Got'ya. All right, we'll be back soon." He kissed her on the lips so tenderly that Amanda dropped her eyes in embarrassment, but Robbie smiled.

"He's really gone on her," Robbie said as Pink Pig, Amanda, and he started off ahead of Brown Knight. "I guess he's found *his* princess."

"They're being careless," Pink Pig said. "Dark Knight never goes anywhere without his sword. And where was Brown Knight's sword?"

"Whoops," Brown Knight said. He'd come up behind them in time to hear. "Be right back. I left it behind a tree somewhere." He strode off and soon returned. His legs were so long and muscular that he hadn't even had to run to catch up with them.

Peasant Man and Woman were loading potatoes into a wooden cart.

"Some pile of spuds you've got there. Want us to bring them over to the dragon for you?" Brown Knight asked.

Peasant Man kept on loading potatoes, too deaf to hear, but Peasant Woman looked at Brown Knight in terror.

"Don't worry," Pink Pig explained to her. "He's come to take over the castle from Dark Knight and bring peace to the Little World."

Peasant Woman began gesturing rapidly at Pink Pig. When she stopped, Pink Pig turned to Amanda and Brown Knight and said, "They dig potatoes from dawn till dark to feed Dragon, and they're afraid if they stop, Dragon will burn their cottage down."

"No kidding! They must get pretty tired of keeping up with that big lizard's appetite," Brown Knight said.

Peasant Woman wiped tears from her eyes and nodded, holding her back as if it ached.

"Well, you can rest now," Brown Knight said. "With the help of my trusty army here, we're going to turn that dragon into a pussy cat."

"But how?" Robbie asked.

"No problem," Brown Knight said. "While you guys wait in the woods, I'll just roll these spuds on over and cozy up to the big fellow."

"But it might attack you. You're a stranger here," Pink Pig said.

"Then I lop its head off." Brown Knight whipped his sword around to show how easy it would be. Peasant Woman ducked and pulled her husband back.

"Did you ever kill a dragon before?" Robbie asked.

"Well, not exactly," Brown Knight admitted.

"The dragon's pretty old and doesn't see too well, but it can smell you," Pink Pig said.

"Maybe if you rub your hands with dirt and wear Peasant Man's shirt—" Amanda suggested.

"Now that's a smart girl," Brown Knight said.

He immediately rubbed himself with earth. Then he traded shirts with the bewildered Peasant Man, who was reassured by his wife that all was well. Brown Knight's leather vest hung comically to the old man's knees.

"I'm coming with you," Robbie said and quickly dabbed some dirt on himself, too.

"The dragon may be old and blind, but he's still dangerous," Pink Pig warned.

"Someone has to go with Brown Knight in case anything goes wrong," Robbie said. "Like if he drops his sword or someone comes up behind him."

"There's my brave buddy!" Brown Knight laid his hand approvingly on Robbie's shoulder and Robbie glowed. Then Brown Knight grasped the cart handles. "Well, let's do it." He pushed off so fast that Robbie had to scramble after him.

Amanda and Pink Pig trotted after the dragon feeders but stopped at the edge of the woods to watch from a distance. They saw the dragon sleeping in the shade of the castle wall. "It's so big and ugly," Amanda whispered to Pink Pig.

"That's what it's supposed to be," Pink Pig said. "As dragons go, ours isn't bad looking."

Still Amanda held her breath when Brown Knight and Robbie closed in on it, and she gasped when the dragon lifted its head and sniffed the air. Slowly it rose. A thin tongue of flame flicked from its mouth. That didn't stop Brown Knight from shoving the cart close and overturning it so that the potatoes rolled out in a heap under the dragon's nose. It swung its head back and forth and steam began to rise from the potatoes.

"What's it doing," Amanda whispered, "burning them up?"

"Cooking them," Pink Pig said.

No sooner had the dragon finished its cooking, than it started gobbling the steaming-hot potatoes. "Ouch!" Amanda said.

"Dragon's got a fireproof mouth," Pink Pig said.

Robbie and Brown Knight waited as the pile of potatoes disappeared with amazing speed. Then Brown Knight dared to reach out an earth-stained hand to the dragon's long greenish neck. At his touch, the beast reared back in alarm. Out shot a torch that burned Brown Knight's hand. He began hopping up and down, waving his hand about. Robbie went running off, but he returned at once dragging the sword which Brown Knight had apparently left behind somewhere again.

"Not yet!" Pink Pig said even though Robbie was too far away to hear her.

Brown Knight must have said something similar because Robbie quickly hid the sword again.

"Lucky thing that dragon's so blind, or he'd have turned Robbie into a potato chip," Pink Pig said.

They saw Robbie heaving the sword into the cart. He took one of the cart's handles and Brown Knight took the other, sparing his burned hand which he kept blowing on while they trundled the cart across the field toward the woods. Behind them, the dragon settled down to nap in the shade again.

"It doesn't look like the dragon's too easy to tame," Amanda said. "We'll have to think of something else besides potatoes."

"You will," Pink Pig said. "You've got the best ideas." Her black-speck eyes shone with pride in Amanda.

That night, before she went to sleep, Amanda tried to think. While Ballerina was cooling Brown Knight's hand in the stream, everyone had looked to Amanda to suggest what they should do next, but nothing had occurred to her.

"We might as well keep feeding the dragon. It'll save those peasant folk some work anyway," Brown Knight said.

"I guess so," Amanda had said.

They'd left it at that and returned to their own world. Now there were two menaces Amanda had to figure out how to get around, the dragon and Angel. It was a toss-up as to which was the more dangerous.

nine

Amanda woke up from a dream about the Little World overcome by terror. The dragon had inflated to gargantuan size. But then it floated off like a harmless balloon with the vapor trail of its fiery breath strung out behind it.

Pink Pig lay snuggled in her hand. "Don't worry so much, Amanda. You'll think of something," Pink Pig said.

"But nothing's right," Amanda fretted. It wasn't just the Little World or what Angel was doing to Robbie. It was a black hole in her chest that friends had once filled, and Dale and Pearly. Here in L.A. there was just Mother, and she was unhappy, too.

Amanda could hear her voice pleading with someone on the telephone—Tony probably. She didn't sound like the self-confident mother of old. Sometimes she'd been critical and unsympathetic, but she'd given Amanda a sense of security that was now gone.

"Want to keep me company in school today, Pink

Pig?" Amanda asked as she pulled on her blue-flowered pants.

"I like being with you anywhere," Pink Pig said.

That comforted Amanda enough so that she kissed her friend's soft snout and went off to the kitchen to get her cereal, juice, and milk.

Mother was still on the phone. Her slender fingers nervously twisted the blue beads that matched her shoes and made a bright line on her plain, pearl-gray dress.

"I like your beads, Mother," Amanda said when the call was over.

"Tony can be so cruel." Mother spoke as if she hadn't heard the compliment. She picked up her cold toast and put it down without taking a bite. "Telling me it was a young party, and I wouldn't fit in. I should tell him *he* doesn't fit in my life anymore."

"Why don't you?"

"Because I've lost my pride," Mother snapped.

"You like him that much?"

Mother folded in her lower lip, considering. "It seems I must."

"But if he makes you unhappy—"

"Oh, Amanda! I'm just annoyed that he's put off our date again, and I know he never mentioned being invited to any party even though he says he told me about it."

"Maybe you really *wouldn't* like the party."

"You don't understand. Without Tony, my life's just work, work, work. I need to have something to look forward to. Someone."

Wasn't *she* someone to look forward to? Amanda

thought with brief resentment. But she knew she'd never been enough for Mother. Dale had been, before he joined the army. He'd kept Mother entertained and busy planning his future. "Dale's coming home soon," Amanda reminded her.

"I know. And you and Dale mean everything to me, but—I'm basically a selfish woman. Children are a responsibility. A man, a friend my own age—that's different."

Amanda nodded. "Like if I didn't have Robbie, I'd hate it here."

Mother frowned. "You mean because of that girl downstairs? I spoke to Moira, and she promised to make Angel apologize. Apparently Angel's terribly disturbed that her father's left them. She's lashing out at everyone. . . . But, Amanda, you've made a friend in school, haven't you?"

"Just to eat lunch with. She doesn't like me much. And I don't like the way she says mean things about people."

"You don't have to stick with her if she's nasty."

Amanda shrugged, wondering why, if Mother thought that way, she stuck with Tony. But Amanda knew better than to wonder such a thing aloud.

"Well, off to work," Mother said more cheerfully. She surprised Amanda with a kiss and said, "I'm glad you're here, darling."

The kiss and the words lifted Amanda's spirits.

The instant she sat down next to Robbie on the school bus, he started talking about the dragon. "We could dig a pit in the field and put potatoes in and lead the dragon so it'd fall in, and then we could make like a cage top to keep it there," Robbie said. He'd obviously been thinking hard.

Amanda lifted Pink Pig from her pocket and asked her what she thought.

"Who's going to dig a pit big enough to catch that dragon?" Pink Pig asked, remaining unobtrusively tiny in the palm of Amanda's hand.

"He is pretty big," Robbie admitted. "As big as an elephant maybe. Anyway, let's ask Brown Knight what he thinks."

"I doubt Brown Knight's much of a planner," Pink Pig said.

Robbie laughed. "Even if he was, he's so gone on Ballerina, he can't think of anything else." A small face peered at them from the seat in front of them. "Hi," Robbie greeted the little boy who looked like a first grader. The child immediately faced front and slid down so that they couldn't see him anymore.

Robbie grinned at Amanda and whispered, "Shy."

Amanda smiled back, not thinking further about the first grader until they got off the bus. Then she noticed him talking to Angel.

"Robbie, look."

"Oh oh." Robbie had picked up on Amanda's suspicion fast. "Do you think he was a spy?"

"Who knows? With Angel, anything's possible."

* * *

That afternoon, they hung back, only getting off the bus after Angel had disappeared into her house. Then they made a dash for the garage. But in the dim light of

109

the garage, they saw Angel blocking the stairs to Amanda's apartment. She must have raced through her house and out the kitchen door.

"You're not getting in," she said, folding her arms like bars across her chest.

"It's my apartment," Amanda said. "You can't keep me out."

"Just try and get past me."

"Angel, what do you want?" Amanda asked.

Angel's triumphant grin transformed into a pleading look. "I wanna play with you."

"But we don't want to play with you," Amanda said, wishing her mother could hear how firm she sounded, or her brother who liked to call her Mouse.

"You're doing a game with a brown knight and a pink pig. I can do that. You could teach me," Angel said.

"That little kid *was* a spy, wasn't he?" Robbie said. "What'd you pay him for spying, Angel?"

"Nothing. I just told him I'd give him his lunch pail back."

"You're such a bully," Amanda said.

Ignoring the insult, Angel whined, "Come on, let me play. I'm sorry I hit you, Amanda, and I'm sorry I fooled around with Robbie like that. Let me play. I'll be nice from now on if you give me a chance. Please!"

Robbie and Amanda turned toward each other questioningly. How should they handle this? "The Little World is a special place," Amanda said slowly. "Not everybody can come in. Only who Pink Pig lets in, and she probably wouldn't let *you*."

"Why not?" Angel asked.

"You get what you want by pushing people around, Angel. Pink Pig wouldn't like that," Amanda said.

"Who is Pink Pig?" Angel wanted to know.

"Just a miniature my grandma once gave me."

"Pink Pig's magic," Robbie blurted out.

Amanda expected Angel to start laughing and announce that *she* didn't believe in magic. Instead, she begged, "Can I see her?"

"No." Amanda was alarmed. Pink Pig was no bigger than the tip of Angel's thumb. One toss and Angel would have her over the garden wall and gone forever. "I can't trust you."

"Yes, you can. I'll promise. I promise on my honor that I won't do anything bad so long as you let me play with you."

"On your honor?" Robbie scoffed. "What good's that, Angel?"

"You'd have to promise on your father's life for us to believe you," Amanda said.

Angel looked shocked. "I won't do that."

"Why not if you're going to be good and aren't just tricking us?"

"I'm not, but . . . my daddy . . ." Angel looked down at her feet and fidgeted. "All right," she said reluctantly. "All right. You got me. I promise on my daddy's life that I'll be good and not push anybody around."

"From now on, never again," Amanda insisted.

"From now on, never again," Angel repeated dutifully.

111

Amanda unlocked the door. It felt uncomfortable to be letting Angel inside her safe place. It was taking a risk even with Angel's promise, but if they were being foolish to trust her, Pink Pig wouldn't let her in the Little World, and that would be that.

Amanda set Pink Pig down in the middle of the kitchen table. Solemnly, Angel and Robbie took positions at either end. "This is Angel," Amanda said to her precious companion. "She wants to come into the Little World. What do you think?"

Amanda was surprised when she heard Angel gasp and saw her eyes widen in awe. Pink Pig had come alive, still miniature, but with her rubbery flesh quivering and her black eyes pulsing with intelligence.

"Gah!" said Angel. She looked petrified.

"We have enough trouble in the Little World right now without letting that girl in," Pink Pig said. "The dark knight's returning."

"Really!" Amanda exclaimed. "Does Brown Knight know?"

"Brown Knight pays no attention to anything but Ballerina," Pink Pig said.

"But what if that dark knight catches him without his sword? I better go help him," Robbie said.

"What about me?" Angel squeaked, suddenly recovering her power of speech. "If there's gonna be a fight, I'll help. I'm good at fighting."

Amanda and Robbie looked at Pink Pig. "You crossed your fingers," she said to Angel.

"What?" Amanda asked.

"When you made her promise on her father's life to be good, she crossed her fingers."

112

Angel held her hands out with fingers spread and repeated her promise, this time as if she meant it. Satisfied, Pink Pig said, "Hurry then. We're wasting time."

They arrived in the field where Spangled Giraffe was grazing peacefully. "Where are we?" Angel asked.

"Shush. This is the Little World. But we don't have time to explain it now," Pink Pig said.

Under the leafy boughs of a tree, Brown Knight and Ballerina sat entwined in each other's arms. "I don't even see his sword," Pink Pig said with disgust.

"It's over there." Robbie pointed to a cloth bag filled with potato eyes waiting to be planted in the prepared furrows. The hilt of the sword poked from the top of the bag. "I'll get it for him."

"He's got muscles to spare," Angel whispered to Amanda. "Is he the dark knight?"

"No, no," Amanda said. "He's our friend. He'll bring peace to the Little World if he wins. But Dark Knight's got the dragon on his side."

"A dragon!" Angel looked alarmed.

"Well, he's a poor, blind, old dragon," Amanda said. "But he does snort flames that can burn you."

"Wow! And what's Robbie's job?"

"He's Brown Knight's companion, sort of like an assistant."

"Baby face Robbie?" Angel sounded disbelieving.

"Robbie's pretty brave," Amanda said so positively that although Angel appeared doubtful, she didn't argue.

Brown Knight looked up as they approached him. "Hello there, my friends. Brought a new recruit for our army with you?" Grinning, he leaned back on one elbow, his head against Ballerina's slender knee. "She looks pretty tough."

"Yes," Amanda said. "This is Angel. She likes to fight. The dark knight's on his way."

Brown Knight sat up straight. "No fooling? He really is? Well, how about that? Never mind. I'm sick of lugging potatoes to that stupid dragon. It couldn't care less who feeds it. A good fight'll be better." He stood up and stretched his brawny arms against the sky.

"Shouldn't we try to surprise Dark Knight instead of him surprising us?" Robbie asked.

Amanda was nodding and added, "We should ambush him before he can get to his castle and sic his dragon on us."

"Anyone know which direction he's coming from?" Brown Knight asked.

Ballerina's slender arm pointed straight at the hill on which the castle stood. A dark speck was riding down the hill toward them, and now they could hear the thunder of hoofbeats.

"Wow! What a beautiful horse," Angel said.

"That's Wild Horse," Pink Pig said. "He's beautiful but mean."

"I could ride him," Angel boasted. "I bet I could ride him."

"Where'd I leave my sword?" Brown Knight asked. Robbie scooted after it, and Brown Knight ordered, "Ballerina, you go hide in Peasant Man and Woman's hut." He hefted his sword, looking serious. "Kids, you go hide in the woods. If I need you, I'll holler."

"I'm not hiding," Angel said.

"You do what you're told or else," Brown Knight growled at her.

"Okay, okay," she said and followed Amanda and Pink Pig to the woods which were close to that edge of the field.

Robbie stood his ground. "I'm staying with you," he told Brown Knight.

"My good buddy!" Brown Knight slung an arm around Robbie's shoulders, and they turned to face the enemy together.

Dark Knight flew toward them like a vengeful bird of prey. Amanda, Pink Pig, and Angel hurried to hide behind trees.

Brown Knight waited, legs astride, leaning on his sword. "I've come to claim your castle, Dark Knight," he trumpeted, "but let's talk it over before we rush into battle."

In answer, Dark Knight unsheathed his sword and aimed it right at Brown Knight's chest.

Brown Knight leapt nimbly to one side as the dark knight charged him on horseback.

"Now that's not friendly," Brown Knight said. "I was even going to offer to share the castle with you."

Wild Horse wheeled and reared and Dark Knight's sword came down, narrowly missing Brown Knight's head. "I guess you don't believe in sharing," Brown Knight continued as coolly as if he hadn't just been attacked. "Okay for you."

Then his sword flashed, and Dark Knight screamed. From the castle came an answering bellow. The dragon's. Following the sound of its master's voice, it lumbered down the hill at an incredible speed for an old beast.

"Brown Knight'll need help now," Pink Pig said.

"We've got to distract the dragon somehow," Amanda said. "Let's get potatoes from Peasant Man and Woman. Come on, Angel."

They dashed off and were lucky enough to find the old couple loading potatoes into the cart. "We'll bring the cart right back," Amanda said breathlessly. She took one shaft of the half-full cart. Angel grabbed the other, and they raced back to the field with Pink Pig trotting behind them while Amanda explained to Angel, as well as she could, what the potatoes were for.

Brown Knight's arm was bloody, but he was fighting hard. Dark Knight still rode Wild Horse, who was rearing and whinnying and twisting as he tried to kick the agile Brown Knight.

The dragon was crossing the field. "Here fellow, here fellow," Angel yelled, running right at the dragon with the cart in which the potatoes bumped about like popcorn. Whoosh! Out shot an arrow of flame. Angel yelped and dropped the cart. Amanda jumped back, too, but the flame wasn't directed at them but at the potatoes. The dragon was ready for a mid-morning snack. Angel watched, openmouthed, as the dragon calmly cooked its potatoes.

Suddenly Robbie, who'd been staying close to Brown Knight, began throwing rocks he'd collected. "Ow!" the dark knight yelled and pulled off his helmet. Then the most amazing thing happened. A cascade of long dark hair rippled down the dark knight's back. For the

116

first time ever, they could see his face. Only it wasn't a his.

"It's a girl, and she's beautiful!" Amanda said.

"Well, what do you know," Brown Knight said. He lowered his sword. "Now what do I do?" he wondered out loud. "Can't kill a pretty lady."

The dark knight blushed which just made her more beautiful. "Fool," she cried out in a high, sweet voice. She wheeled her horse around and rode off toward the castle.

"No wonder nobody ever heard the dark knight speak," Pink Pig said. "Her voice gives her away."

The dragon finished every single potato, then turned and waddled back toward the castle, leaving the little army alone in the field.

"What now?" Robbie asked.

"Beats me, good buddy," Brown Knight said. "Let's take a break and think it over. After all that jumping around in the hot sun, I'm thirsty. How about you guys?"

"You're wounded," Amanda said.

He looked down at his bloody arm. "It's just a scratch," he said. "I'll go find some moss to soak up the blood."

It seemed to Amanda they'd been gone from the real world a long time. Mother might be getting home from work any minute, and if Amanda wasn't there, she'd be upset. "I think we'd better get back to our own world," Amanda said. "We'll come back later, Brown Knight." She touched Pink Pig who immediately returned them to Amanda's kitchen.

They stood there looking at Angel in silence. Pink

Pig was a rose quartz miniature again, tiny in the middle of the table. Blinking, Angel asked, "Did that really happen?"

"What?" Amanda asked to test her.

"That knight turned into a lady."

"I told you knights could be women sometimes, didn't I?" Robbie asked Amanda. "Like Joan of Arc?"

She nodded, but what impressed her the most was that Angel had really been to the Little World with them.

"You did okay, Robbie," Angel said. "How come you did okay there when you're such a wimp here?"

"I don't know," Robbie said.

"You know what I'd like more than anything in the whole world?" Angel said dreamily.

Amanda couldn't imagine. "What?"

"To ride that wild horse." Her eyes glowed with desire.

We've got her, Amanda realized. Now we've got her in our power.

ten

Angel didn't even ask. She just joined them in the back of the bus on the way home from school as if they were a trio now. Parking her feet in the aisle across from Amanda and Robbie, she pressed forward to talk at them. "I've gotta ride that wild horse. You've gotta bring Pink Pig down to the garden and get me back into the Little World, Amanda."

Amanda shook her head. It made her nervous just to think of bringing Pink Pig into Angel's garden.

"Why not?"

"Because we haven't got time for stuff like that. We're trying to help Brown Knight."

"So we'll help him. That's okay," Angel said, "so long as I get on that horse."

"He'd probably throw you," Robbie said.

"Not me. No way," Angel boasted. "When I was little, my daddy was a stunt rider for a movie, and he taught me to ride. I could ride that wild horse like

119

nothing. I bet he runs like the wind. I bet he's like flying. Oh, please, Amanda!"

"But we don't even know what's happening," Amanda stalled. "I mean, now Brown Knight can't fight the dark knight. So how's he going to take over the Little World?"

"He said he'd share the castle," Angel tossed out. "Don't you remember?"

"That dark knight didn't act like she wanted to share," Amanda said.

"She might attack him again," Robbie said. "And we're his army." He sounded glad about that.

"So? You've gotta go back to the Little World to find out, don't you?" Angel asked.

"What we should do next," Amanda said thoughtfully, "is ask Frog what he thinks."

"Frog?"

"Frog's the one who knows," Robbie explained.

"I want to meet him," Angel said. "Maybe he could tell me how to catch that wild horse."

"He might," Robbie said.

Amanda looked at him. Was he willing to let Angel back into the Little World? It seemed he was. Well, Amanda reasoned, Angel had been a help, and she'd certainly been brave about approaching the dragon with the potatoes. Maybe it would turn out that Wild Horse would tame her instead of the other way around.

"Come on. Don't be mean," Angel begged her, and Robbie looked at Amanda expectantly.

"Okay," she heard herself say. "Okay."

She should have asked Pink Pig, Amanda thought afterward, afterward when it was clear she'd made a terrible mistake. But Robbie had the most reason not to trust Angel, and his willingness had made Amanda feel mean about her suspicions.

"Let me hold Pink Pig," Angel demanded, reaching out her hand the instant Amanda stepped through the garden gate.

"No, I'll hold her."

"Why can't I? Come on, be nice," Angel whined.

"Listen, Angel, you haven't been nice to us," Amanda said. Her face had healed, but she touched the spot where Angel had hit her.

"I know," Angel said surprisingly. "I've got a bad temper. But we're friends now, aren't we?"

The idea of being Angel's friend startled Amanda. Disarmed, the best she could do was mutter, "You better stop being such a bully then."

"Please," Angel begged. "Please, let me hold Pink Pig?"

Amanda regretted it the instant she gave over her friend to the cage of Angel's fingers. Abruptly, Angel turned and retreated to the wall of the garden. There she stood, hunched into herself.

"Take me to the Little World," she commanded Pink Pig.

"She won't take you anywhere unless I ask her," Amanda said.

"Oh, boy," Robbie was muttering anxiously, "oh, boy, oh, boy." He looked as scared as Amanda felt.

121

"You better give her back," she told Angel.

Ignoring Amanda, Angel commanded again, "Take me to see Wild Horse now or you'll be sorry, Pig."

Nothing happened for a long minute except that Angel's jaw clenched and her face swelled with anger.

"Angel," Robbie said. "Let Amanda do it. She'll get you there if you give Pink Pig back to her."

"Shut up, you. What do you know!" Angel's eyes glared at Robbie. "Take me now or else," she commanded the miniature.

"She won't hurt Pink Pig, will she?" Amanda whispered to Robbie.

"I'm sorry, Amanda," Robbie cried. "It's my fault. I should've known not to trust her."

"Well, Pink Pig's never going to let her in the Little World anyway," Amanda said to calm him.

"Shut up!" Angel screamed. "Shut up, you two. Stop talking behind my back, or I'll throw this stupid pig over the wall."

Fear struck Amanda with a cold fist. Beyond the wall where Angel stood was the canyon. Pink Pig would be lost forever in that canyon. Amanda couldn't even get there to search, and even if she did somehow, she'd never find a morsel of pink quartz amidst all the small stones and scrubby outcroppings.

"I thought you wanted to get back into the Little World so much," Amanda said to Angel. "You won't get there if you don't give Pink Pig back to me."

"And you won't either," Angel said. It was amazing how different she looked now that she had the upper hand. She'd gone from pleading to sneering, from an ordinary girl to a hateful one.

"Give me Pink Pig, and I'll ask her to help you ride that horse," Amanda bargained.

Angel glowered at her in answer. Amanda repeated her offer. She was so intent on persuading Angel that she forgot Robbie was in the garden, too. Suddenly, her eye caught a movement in the bushes beside Angel's legs. The next instant Robbie leaped out and flung himself at Angel.

His attack was unexpected. Amanda stood frozen, watching the struggle, until she realized that Angel was hurting him. She had him helpless on his back, and she was pummeling him with her fists. Then Amanda rushed across the grass and grabbed Angel's arms. The solid arms were slippery, and when Amanda's thin fingers lost their grip, Angel turned to attack her.

Amanda slithered behind the nearest bush and snaked along, getting scratched by sticks and thorns, but she figured they had to be less painful than what would happen to her if Angel caught her.

"Ouch!" Angel yelped. Robbie was biting her leg.

They'd lose fighting fair, Amanda thought, and they couldn't afford to lose this time. She detoured between two bushes, grabbed Angel's jungly hair, and yanked. "Yeow!" Angel shouted. She pulled loose from both of them and jumped on the trunk of the only tree of any size in the garden. Its branches overhung the top of the wall overlooking the canyon. Angel shinnied up the tree and climbed onto the wall.

"Now try and get me," she taunted them.

"You better get down," Robbie said. "You'll kill yourself if you fall off there."

"But I won't fall," Angel said. "See?" She got up slowly and balanced on the wall.

It made Amanda sick to think of that sheer precipice. "Angel, please come down," she begged. Awful as the girl was, it would be terrible if she fell.

"Now watch this," Angel said and raised her clenched fist. It still held Pink Pig.

Robbie screamed, "Don't, Angel. Please, please, don't. I'll give you anything you want. Don't throw Pink Pig."

Terror choked Amanda. In her mind she could see Pink Pig falling, a tiny pink pebble disappearing into the bits of gravel and tufts of grass on the impossibly sheer wall of the canyon.

"Angel." The man's voice was hard. "Get your fat butt down here."

Amanda nearly fainted with relief. The man had sinewy arms that snaked out from a pink plaid shirt and hair slicked back above a bony face. His eyes were slits of anger, and his lips had disappeared into a thin line.

"Daddy!" Angel chimed sweetly. "Daddy, you're home."

"What are you doing up there, you little hellion?"

"Just—they were teasing me; so I was showing them—"

His eyes examined Amanda and Robbie. "Looks like you got in your licks before they got you, Angel. I said get down. What're you doing?"

She leaped back into the garden. "Nothing, Daddy."

"Where's your mother?"

"I don't know. At the bank maybe." She approached him cautiously.

"You want to come with me?" he asked her.

"Oh, yes, Daddy."

"Get your things then and let's go."

Angel gasped, and without another word ran into the house as if afraid he might change his mind.

"She's got my miniature!" Amanda cried.

"That's your tough luck, kid," the man said as he turned and followed Angel into the house.

*   *   *

"At least she didn't throw Pink Pig," Robbie tried to console Amanda.

Amanda shook her head. So long as Angel had the miniature in her possession, Pink Pig was in danger. Small as she was, she could be hidden anywhere. Amanda tortured herself by thinking up good hiding places: in the pocket of an old jacket at the back of a closet, inside the flour container, under a pile of towels, in a toy box. A million places would do to hide the magic rose quartz miniature, a million places where she'd never be found again.

"I'm going upstairs to read," Amanda said. She needed to be alone.

"Okay," Robbie sounded unsure. "I'll see you later."

Upstairs, Amanda wandered around the apartment aimlessly, unable after all to settle down to reading. Finally, she sat down and wrote Pearly a letter about all that had happened in the real world with Angel and Pink Pig and Robbie. Pearly would sympathize. Probably she'd offer to buy another miniature, not that that would help, but at least Pearly would feel bad for her.

At six o'clock Mother called. "Darling, I'm sorry. I know I should have been home half an hour ago, but

125

something's come up and—could you eat dinner alone tonight? We have leftover chicken on the second shelf in the refrigerator that—"

"Okay, Mother. I know."

"And don't wait up for me. I may be very late. You won't be scared alone?"

"No, I'll be okay." She wasn't being brave. Losing Pink Pig had left her with a numbness that Mother's presence wouldn't melt.

The phone rang again as soon as Amanda put the receiver down.

"Amanda?"

"Dale!" Amanda yelled. "Hi, how are you?"

"Fine, I'm coming home on leave this weekend. Just wanted to let you and Ma know so you don't make other plans. I'm taking you to Disneyland, right?"

"I can't wait to see you, Dale. I missed you so much."

"Me too, Little Mouse. I miss you a whole bunch. You doing okay in sunny California?"

"Sort of."

"Sort of doesn't sound so good. . . . Well, you'll tell me when you see me, right?"

"Right."

"Okay, let me speak to Ma."

"She's out, Dale."

"Out? How come? Is she leaving you alone a lot?"

"No, just tonight. She's got a boyfriend."

"I know. Sounds pretty heavy." A buzzing sound interrupted their conversation. Dale said, "Listen kid, I gotta go. Love you."

126

"I love you, too," she said.

It was amazing how much better Dale's phone call made her feel. All at once getting Pink Pig back began to seem possible. Tomorrow, or whenever Angel's father brought her back, Amanda would try to negotiate with her, offer her something she wanted even more than Pink Pig. Somehow Angel would be persuaded.

The knock on the door made Amanda jump even though she guessed it was Robbie by the familiar rhythm.

It was a different Robbie who stepped into her apartment. He sparkled with excitement. "I got to tell you what happened, Amanda. My dad called. He's coming to get me and take me to see my mother tomorrow."

"Really? That's wonderful."

"Well, maybe. The thing is Mom's real sick. Dad says she wants to see me, but then he's going to bring me back here because I can't stay in intensive care for more than ten minutes, and he doesn't want me sitting around the waiting room so much. I guess I won't be gone more than a day. He's even letting me skip school. He's *never* let me skip school before."

"I hope she gets well soon, Robbie. Maybe seeing you will help her."

"Yeah, I hope so. That's what my dad thinks, I guess, or he wouldn't be taking me out of school." Robbie was so excited he couldn't stop grinning. "I want to draw something to take her as a present. Do you have paper I could borrow? I didn't get a new pad yet."

Amanda couldn't find any real drawing paper, but Robbie accepted a few sheets of Mother's typing paper

127

and said that would do. "You want to work up here?" Amanda asked. "My mother's not coming home yet."

"No, I gotta wait for Moira. Angel's father told me to tell her he's taking Angel for a vacation."

"Really? Where to?"

"He didn't say. Boy, was she happy. I asked her to give Pink Pig back, but she wouldn't. I asked her in front of her father, but he didn't pay any attention."

"He didn't care that she stole it," Amanda said. "He's not nice."

"I didn't like him either," Robbie said. "Angel sure likes him though."

"My brother's coming. He's taking me to Disneyland," Amanda said.

"Lucky you," Robbie said. "I guess we both have something to be happy about today. And Angel, too."

Except that Pink Pig's gone, Amanda thought.

Robbie left with the paper, and Amanda fixed her supper. She'd cleaned up and was thinking about making cookies for Dale when she heard her mother's key in the door.

It was earlier than Amanda had expected her. "Hi," Amanda said. "Guess who called?"

"Tony?" Mother asked hopefully.

"Dale," Amanda said.

"Oh . . . that's nice."

"He's coming home on leave this weekend."

"How wonderful." Mother's smile took such effort that it didn't make it past her lips.

"What's wrong, Mother?"

"Tony's just informed me he doesn't want to see me

128

anymore, Amanda. He says he doesn't want a full-time relationship, and I make him feel guilty when he—" Mother sat down in the nearest chair and turned her face away. Amanda came close and began patting her shoulder timidly, not sure that Mother wanted her shoulder patted, but Mother grabbed her hand and held on.

"I'm so stupid, Amanda. I knew from the beginning that he was too young for me. . . . My skin's going bad. What's a young man want with a wrinkled, saggy-skinned old woman?"

"But you're not old, Mother, and you're still beautiful."

Mother squeezed her hand. "Nothing's ever worked out for me, nothing I've ever tried, nothing I've ever dreamed about."

"I'm sorry."

"Oh, Amanda, you're really such a dear child. Have I told you how glad I am you're here?"

"Yes, you have, and I know you like me better than you did."

Mother gasped and embraced her hard enough to suffocate her. Amanda thought she understood; it was because Mother was feeling so bad about Tony. It was fine, Amanda thought, that she'd finally gotten old enough to give her mother some comfort, the kind of comfort only Dale had had the power to give her before. And it was great that Dale was coming. But oh, she wished she hadn't handed Pink Pig over to Angel, just handed her over—and to *Angel*.

129

_____ *eleven*

Neither Robbie nor Angel was on the school bus when Amanda got on the next morning. She knew where Robbie was. She'd seen him drive off with his father. It should make him feel better to see his mother, and he only had another couple of months to survive with Angel before rejoining his parents for good. Amanda was glad for his sake, but sorry for herself. She'd really miss Robbie. Idly, she wondered where Angel's father had taken her. Moira's car hadn't been in the garage this morning so she must not be home either.

School was comfortably routine. Amanda got a 94 on a math test she'd been worried about, but she got a disappointing B on her composition on pets. She'd written about Flopsy and Mopsy. Pearly's rabbits were Amanda's only experience with pets since Mother had never allowed her to have any. It hadn't been a very inspired composition, Amanda admitted to herself after listening to one the teacher shared with them about a cat that always chose cat haters' laps to sit on. Amanda wished she could write something that funny.

At noontime, she sat down at her usual lunch table space and waited for Megan to plunk her tray down across from her. There she came with her tray, but to Amanda's surprise, Megan walked past her without a word and sat down with a pair of fat blond twins. The three of them had been working on an art project for days, but why hadn't Megan said she was going to eat with the twins? Maybe she was afraid Amanda would ask to join them. That hurt. Amanda felt as if she were being shed like an outgrown skin. Well, she and Megan had never been more than convenient company for each other. Still, Amanda dragged through the rest of the day feeling like a reject. She sat alone again on the bus going home.

"Hi, Mouse," Dale greeted her at the door.

"Dale!" Amanda screeched. The day's miseries disappeared instantly in the joy of seeing him.

He picked her up and whirled her around as if she were a toy, then set her down and looked her over. While he was looking, she checked him out. Her big brother had turned into a man in the six months that he'd been in the army. He'd always looked like Mother with the same high cheekbones and vivid blue eyes, but now his hollows had filled out. "You look so good," Amanda said.

"Hey, who's talking. I can't call you Little Mouse anymore. You got too pretty."

"I'm not pretty."

"Are you kidding? You're a living doll." He held up

his hand to swear it. "I kid you not." Then he kissed her nose and said, "Come help me eat the quart of pistachio ice cream I bought—Mom never does keep anything good in the freezer—and tell me how things are going."

"Are you really taking me to Disneyland tomorrow?"

"Definitely."

"Could I bring a friend?"

He smiled. "A kid?"

"Yes, Robbie, the boy who's staying downstairs. He's gone to visit his mother in the hospital today, but he'll be back tonight. He's nice."

"If you like him, he must be. . . . How's Mom doing, Amanda?"

"Okay, except that man ditched her last night. He never was all that nice to her. He kept breaking appointments, and she was always . . . I think she's better off without him."

"Yeah, but poor Mom. She's got no luck with the men in her life."

Amanda was telling him about how Mother had taken her to Malibu when they were interrupted by a strange noise. "There it is again," Dale said.

"What?" Amanda asked. She listened. It sounded like wailing.

"Is there an animal caged up somewhere around here?" Dale asked.

Amanda shook her head. "Unless something's wrong with Angel," she said.

"We'd better check it out," Dale said. When he stood up, Amanda followed him.

The wailing was louder in the garage. Dale pounded on the Delaneys' kitchen door. "What's wrong? Do you need help?" he yelled.

Silence. "It's me, Amanda," Amanda called. "My brother's with me. Are you all right?"

The kitchen door opened. It hadn't been Angel who'd been wailing, but her mother. Moira Delaney's face was lumpy and pale. "Amanda," she said, "you could help me. Would you call Angel? She might listen to you. She's been so happy since you two became friends."

"Angel'd never listen to me," Amanda said slowly. She didn't have the heart to tell Moira that Angel was no friend.

"Her father's got her," Moira said. "He wants money or he won't give her back to me. I have an inheritance from my aunt, but that's what I've been living on, and if I give it to him—"

"You better not give him anything," Dale butted in to advise as if he had a right. "You better go to the police."

"I can't," Moira said. "Angel would never forgive me if I sent the police after her father."

"Then what are you going to do?" Amanda asked.

Moira put her fist against her mouth and moaned. "I don't know."

"Maybe there's a friend, somebody he'd listen to?" Dale suggested. "Or his relatives?"

Moira's eyes brightened. "He'd listen to my father. He respects my father." She sniffed. "I never told Delaney my father tried to persuade me not to marry him.

133

Dad was right. He's always been right, but I wouldn't listen to him because he told me calling myself a poet was foolish and I'd never make a living at it. He was right about that, too."

"You should call your father and ask him to help," Dale told her.

She nodded, considered, and nodded some more. Then she smiled at Dale and said, "You must think I'm some kind of a nut." Gently, she touched Amanda's cheek. "And you have such a lovely sister. Amanda's been good for Angel. . . . Well . . . thank you for coming down. You've been a help, both of you." The social smile began to look more natural on her face as she grew calmer. "I'd invite you in, but . . . perhaps I'd better try to reach my father now. It's later in Wisconsin."

"What's with this Angel kid?" Dale asked when he and Amanda were back upstairs.

"She took Pink Pig. And she's rotten mean to Robbie, or she was before—"

"Before what?"

"Before we let her in the Little World."

"Mouse, I mean, Amanda, you're not still hung up on that fantasy stuff, are you?"

"Well," Amanda tried to explain, "Pink Pig brought Robbie and me along into the Little World to help because Brown Knight's come to claim Wizard's castle. See, Wizard promised it to him because Brown Knight helped Wizard once and—but the dark knight turned out to be a girl—"

Dale halted her by cupping his hand over her mouth. "Whoah! Forget it. I can't keep up. I never could keep

134

up with your imagination. . . . And this Robbie goes along with you? No wonder you like him. You're two of a kind."

"Angel went too."

"Into that Little World?"

"Yes. She wants to ride Wild Horse more than anything. She stole Pink Pig from me and she—then she climbed up on the garden wall, and that's when her father came home. He was mad at her."

"For climbing on the wall?"

"She would have been killed if she'd fallen off. The wall's right over the canyon, Dale."

"No kidding. This is some apartment Mom picked! Stuck off here by itself, it's weird even for L.A. No wonder you're back to fantasy land."

Mother got home and embraced Dale. "I see you didn't lose the key I gave you," she said.

"Aren't you surprised to see me?" He sounded disappointed.

"Moira Delaney met me in the garage on her way out, and she told me all about my wonderful children. It seems Angel's been kidnapped by her father?"

"Sort of," Dale said. "At least from what your landlady said. He's holding their kid for ransom." Dale shook his head in disgust.

"Well, she took your advice and called her family," Mother said, "and it seems Moira's father dealt with her husband. I don't know what the father promised him, but Moira's on her way to pick Angel up."

"Good," Dale said. "Now we got that straightened out, I'm going to give *you* some advice, Mom."

"What's that?"

"Find another apartment. This place gives me the creeps. It's bad news for Amanda."

"Well, it may not be ideal, but it's what I can afford, Dale," Mother said. "And have you seen how large and airy the rooms are?"

"Mom, the neighborhood matters more than how the place looks inside," Dale said.

Mother turned to Amanda. "You like your room, don't you, darling?"

"It's okay," Amanda said.

"Certainly it's nicer than what you had with Pearly."

"But with Pearly I had a lot of friends and the animals, and I could walk or ride someplace," Amanda said honestly. "I didn't have to stay inside like here."

"But—" Mother began.

"Listen," Dale interrupted, "if finding another place is such a hassle for you, I'll help."

"How?"

"Well, I'll have more time now I've got this new assignment. I'll find you an apartment, get some of my buddies, rent a U-haul trailer, and move you out. All you'll have to do is pack your clothes and the dishes. How's that?"

"Amanda's just getting used to her new school," Mother said. "It's not a good time to move."

"I don't mind," Amanda hastened to say. "Robbie's my only friend here, and he's leaving soon."

"Where is Robbie?" Mother asked fretfully. Her sudden interest in him gave her an excuse to change the subject. She glanced toward their living room as if he might be hiding in a corner.

"Robbie's seeing his mother at the hospital today. He should be back tonight," Amanda said.

"Uh-oh, we better leave a note on the door downstairs and tell him to come up here in case your landlady doesn't get back in time," Dale said. "Be right back." He left them sitting at the kitchen table.

Mother sighed and then said tartly, "He certainly takes over, doesn't he? I'm surprised the army hasn't made him a commander. Amazing that six months should make such a difference in a boy."

"Well, he's helping us."

"Umm. But I'm used to being boss of my own life. I'm not sure I like being directed." Then she smiled. "Hasn't he gotten handsome, though? . . . Did he like your new haircut, Amanda?"

"I guess so. He said I'm pretty now."

Mother nodded with satisfaction, as if all was right with her world now that she not only had a handsome son but a pretty daughter.

A car stopping outside sent them to Mother's bedroom window in time to see Robbie and his father getting out of the red compact. Robbie's father was bald, but his face was young and amiable. He rang the Delaneys' front doorbell. Dale came out of the garage and intercepted him. Amanda ran down to help him explain. After all, Robbie's father had never met Dale.

". . . so," Dale said after he'd finished telling about Angel and her parents, "Robbie's welcome to stay with us tonight, and Amanda would like him to come to Disneyland with us tomorrow, if that's all right with you."

Mr. Morrison looked dazed. "Disneyland? I suppose. . . But his mother's very ill, very . . . Tonight's

137

crucial the doctors say." He looked at Robbie with concern and continued, "I'll be by her bedside all night. . . . Actually, it would be good for Robbie to be with friends if . . ." Mr. Morrison's eyes brimmed with tears, but he shook them away and cleared his throat. "If she makes it through the night, she's got a good chance according to the doctors."

Robbie choked and ducked his head. His father drew him close and said, "They told us to go out and get a bite to eat, but we didn't feel like eating. I thought it would be best if I brought Robbie home. I had no idea that—" He looked up at the house as if it should have revealed something to him. "This can't have been much of a home. You should have told us, Robbie."

"But you said I should be brave!"

His father winced and touched Robbie's downy hair. "You are brave, son. The way you didn't flinch when you saw your mother with all those tubes, the way you made her smile—I was *very* proud of you."

"She'll be all right. You'll see," Robbie said.

"Let's hope so. Do you want to stay with Amanda's family tonight?"

"If I can't be at the hospital, yeah."

"Look," Dale said confidently, "don't worry about Robbie. We'll take care of him. But you should have the phone number so if you want to call—anybody got a pencil?"

Robbie's father had a pen and pad in his pocket. He wrote down the number, then hugged his son. "I'll be back for you as soon as—as soon as we know, and then we'll get you away from the Delaneys for good, okay?"

138

Robbie nodded, frowning. Amanda took his hand and led him upstairs. Mother suggested she give Robbie her bed and move her pajamas and toothbrush and slippers into Mother's room. Dale could sleep on the couch in the living room. Robbie flopped onto the bed and rolled into the pillow as if he were too exhausted to stay upright another minute. Amanda left him to sleep and went into the living room.

"Chinese take out tonight?" Dale asked Mother.

"Fine."

"I'll go for it," he said. "Amanda, you want to come with me?"

"I better stay here in case Robbie needs me," Amanda said.

"I'll go for the food," Mother said quickly. "I know this area better than you do. You stay with the children, Dale."

"Got you." Dale ambled over to the TV and turned it on. "Anything in the house for snacks, Amanda? Nachos would be good right now."

"I think there's rice crackers," Amanda said and went to get them for him. She thought back to the morning when it had seemed odd that neither Robbie nor Angel was on the bus. What a stormy lot of trouble they'd both been through today. Amanda tried to imagine how Robbie must be feeling. Suppose it was her mother near death. She couldn't even imagine anything that awful. But at least he had a good father. She could tell Robbie that living with just one parent wasn't bad, once you were used to it anyway. Still, Amanda hoped that his mother didn't die tonight.

"Come keep me company," Dale said when she handed him the crinkly package of rice crackers. He patted the couch, and she settled down beside him happily. "How's Pearly doing?" he asked.

"Fine. Pearly's always fine."

"Yeah, I'm glad you have somebody in the family you can count on to be okay."

"I can count on you and Mother, Dale."

"Can you? You able to talk to Mother about yourself now?"

"A little."

He looked at her seriously. "I'm going to try and be there for you more from now on, M—Amanda."

"You can call me Mouse." She smiled. "I kind of like that you have a pet name for me."

His grin was warm. "You know something? If I ever have a kid, I want it to be just like you." He put his arm around her shoulders. She snuggled against him, feeling wonderfully safe while the cops and robbers raced around shooting at each other on the TV.

Mother came back with their dinner, and they ate and talked some more about places they could move to. Amanda thought about moving again. She'd have to start new in another school, but it might be better than this one. There could be someone nicer to eat lunch with. There could be friends for her in another school.

Just before she fell asleep, she started thinking about where Angel could have put Pink Pig. Right now, Pink Pig could be downstairs with Angel in her bedroom. And tomorrow, Amanda could go to work on getting her friend back. Would Angel be glad to be with Moira

140

again, Amanda wondered, or would she rather have stayed with her father? It was hard to have people you loved in all different places. Like Pearly was in New York, and Dale was in the army, and Pink Pig . . . Rotten as she could be, Amanda felt sorry for Angel.

Before she closed her eyes, Amanda cheered herself up by remembering that tomorrow was the trip to Disneyland with Dale and Robbie. That had to be a fun day.

_____ twelve

Amanda popped out of bed and got dressed, so excited about the big day with Dale that she could barely buckle her sandals. Mother was still sound asleep, but she always slept late on Saturdays. The disappointment was finding Dale still sleeping on the living room couch. No wonder. According to the kitchen clock, it was only six a.m. Now what could she do? Amanda wondered. She was too wide awake to go back to bed, and anyway, that would disturb Mother. Just in case Robbie was up, Amanda tapped lightly on the door of her own bedroom. He opened the door immediately. He was wearing yesterday's rumpled clothes, and his face was so sad it hurt to look at him.

"I need to brush my teeth," he said.

"Sure. There's the bathroom." Amanda pointed to the door.

"But I don't have a toothbrush. . . . I guess I could use my finger. My father didn't call, did he?"

"I don't think so."

142

"I guess he'd call right away if anything happened." Robbie controlled his trembling lip and added bravely, "If she died." But saying the words switched on the tears automatically.

Amanda yearned to comfort him, but she didn't know how. All she could think to say was, "I'm sorry I don't have an extra toothbrush." She stepped back to let him walk past her to the bathroom. The phone rang while she was standing there waiting. She jumped. Robbie's father! Did she have to answer? Yes, she did.

Just as she had feared, it was Mr. Morrison. "Robbie's brushing his teeth," she said and held her breath.

But Robbie's father sounded cheerful. "Tell him I've got good news, hopeful, at least. His mother got through the night."

"Whew," Amanda said.

She routed Robbie out of the bathroom, and overheard his end of the phone conversation. "Yeah, yeah, yeah," was all he said, but a smile changed his face from down to up. By the time the call ended, he looked radiant. "She didn't die. My mom's going to get well. Isn't that terrific, Amanda?"

"Terrific," Amanda echoed.

Dale raised his head from his pillow to growl, "What are you kids making so much noise about?" But when they told him about Robbie's mother, Dale got up and made them pancakes for breakfast.

"I didn't know you could make pancakes," Amanda said.

"One of the things my girlfriend taught me." Dale sniffed and rubbed his nose. "About the only good thing."

They left for Disneyland in Dale's rented car before Mother got up. "Have fun," she mumbled sleepily.

Robbie's smile lasted all day. He shook hands with Mickey Mouse while Amanda was admiring the castle. They both went on Space Mountain with Dale, but afterwards, when Dale wanted to try the bobsled down the Matterhorn, Amanda said her stomach had been left behind on Space Mountain. She stayed back, while Robbie squared his jaw and followed Dale. All three of them were attacked by pirates on an otherwise peaceful boat ride in the Caribbean. They went undersea past fish-filled reefs of branching coral and down the water-slide. When they got hungry, they stuffed themselves with hamburgers and french fries, and ice cream sundaes that dripped with chocolate syrup, whipped cream, and nuts.

"Boy, Amanda's lucky to have a brother like you," Robbie told Dale on the way home. "Thanks for the most fun day."

"Anytime, Robbie, anytime," Dale said.

Moira Delaney's car was parked in the garage. "I wonder how the kid's doing," Dale said.

Amanda hoped Angel was all right, and that she still had Pink Pig and hadn't gotten rid of her in some horrible place. It was a miracle that Robbie's mother had survived the night. Amanda could only hope that by another miracle Pink Pig had also survived.

Upstairs, Mother greeted them with the news that Robbie's father had called to say he'd taken a motel room near the hospital. "For the two of you, Robbie. He's coming to pick you up soon."

"Have you heard anything from downstairs?" Dale asked.

"No. Moira's car's in the garage. I suppose they're back to normal."

Dale considered. "Maybe I'll go ask if they're all right."

"Dale, they're not your business," Mother said. "You keep away from that family. The father has a nasty look."

"Mom, I just want to check on what happened. Relax."

"It's foolish to get too friendly with neighbors," Mother persisted. "It just makes for trouble."

"You wanted Amanda to be friends with Angel, didn't you?" Dale said.

Mother pressed her lips together and didn't answer.

Dale was downstairs when Robbie's father arrived. He seemed quite relaxed as he explained that he'd be returning Monday to settle accounts with Moira and pick up Robbie's things. "I can't take time for that today. My wife's condition's still critical. Looking better though."

"Robbie, we should say good-bye now," Amanda said. "I mean, I could be in school when you come back Monday." Suddenly, it struck her that she might never see him again. Never. It was like her friends in Schenectady, like Pearly. People kept getting lost from her life.

"But Amanda—" Robbie's eyes were solemn with his own realizations "—who're you going to sit with on the school bus now?"

145

"I don't know." She shrugged. Then she looked at Mother and said, "I hope we move, too."

"But if we both move," Robbie said, "we'll never find each other again."

"Whoa!" his father said. "Let's not get tragic about this separation, kids. The post office will forward mail. . . . Or better yet, let's make a date. Soon as Robbie's mother's well, we'll celebrate, and Amanda can visit us wherever we are. How's that?"

"Of course," Mother said encouragingly.

Mr. Morrison turned to Amanda. "I understand you've been a good friend to Robbie when he needed a good friend most, and I hope you'll visit us often."

"And Robbie's always welcome to come to us," Mother said.

"I'll call you soon," Robbie whispered in Amanda's ear, "so you can tell me if you get Pink Pig back and what happened in the Little World. Okay?" he asked in a normal voice.

"Okay," she agreed. Her gloomy feeling lifted. Saying good-bye was bearable, if she was sure to see him again.

After Robbie and his father left, Mother began getting a meal together, but in a distracted way. She kept fussing about what was keeping Dale and walking to the windows to look for him. "I don't know why he had to get involved. Someone who kidnaps his own child could be dangerous, and who knows, that man might decide to come back here."

"Dale can take care of himself," Amanda tried to reassure her.

"Dale may act like a man, but he's still a boy . . . I

146

should never have assumed you were safe here." Mother stared at her as if she'd never seen Amanda before. "Tell me the truth, darling, are you scared when I leave you home alone?"

"Sometimes." Amanda almost slipped into the old pattern of making light of her difficulties so as not to bother Mother, but this time she stopped herself and said firmly, "I wish we could move, Mother. I really hate being stuck indoors. It's like being locked in a tower or something."

Mother stiffened. "Do you want to go back to Pearly?"

Amanda took her time to think about that. She could say yes, because she'd certainly been happier with Pearly, but here she was with Mother, and that was right. That was where she should be. "No," Amanda said, "I guess I want to be where you are."

Mother let her breath out in a long, relieved sigh, and she said, "Amanda, you're a very strong girl, aren't you?" Without waiting for an answer, she returned to her cooking.

Strong, Amanda thought. Strong was better than pretty, a lot better. Strong was how she was, not how she looked. Warmth poured into the cavernous space Amanda had always longed to fill with Mother's approval. Strong. Yes, that was how she was.

The instant Dale returned, Mother asked, "What took you so long?"

"Mrs. Delaney needed someone to talk to, I guess. She's got it figured out. She's going to let the state take over this property. They've been trying to buy it from her for a while to build a feeder road on. And she'll go back to Wisconsin, to her folks. Her sister'll give her a job in her gift shop, and Angel'll have a pile of cousins there."

"And Angel's father?"

"They're getting divorced. That's part of the deal Mrs. Delaney's father made with him."

"Good," Mother said and added ironically, "Now that you've straightened out their lives, how about helping me straighten out ours."

"What do you mean, Mom?" Dale asked.

"You said you'd help me move. If we can find a place, I'm willing. I don't want to be a bad mother anymore."

"Who said you were?" Dale asked.

Mother didn't say anything, but she looked so distressed that Dale hugged her. "Hey, Mom, you did a good job raising us. I know it wasn't easy earning the money and taking care of everything that went wrong all by yourself, but you did it, and look how well we've come out. Especially Amanda." He winked at his sister. "Isn't she some kid?"

Mother nodded. A rush of sympathy for her sent Amanda running to hug Mother and Dale both. It was a happy moment.

* * *

Sunday, they all got up early to start apartment hunting. Amanda sat in the back seat of the car. Mother drove while she and Dale discussed the newspaper ads and maps and freeway routes and distances from Mother's job to where they could possibly afford to live.

Amanda didn't listen. Her mind was fully occupied

148

with what Angel could have done with the magic miniature. There'd been a kink in Amanda's heart ever since she'd finally gone downstairs to confront Angel yesterday afternoon and Moira had said Angel wasn't feeling well and couldn't talk to her. If Pink Pig were gone forever, it would be worse in a way than losing Robbie. Another friend like him might come along, but never another magic rose quartz pig with black-speck eyes and a corkscrew tail.

And without Pink Pig to take her there, Amanda would never find out what had happened in the Little World. Had Brown Knight married his Ballerina and gotten his castle, and what was the dark knight lady doing? Without Pink Pig, the Little World was lost, too.

"What's the matter, Amanda?" Mother asked as they got out of the car for the fourth time to look at an apartment. "Are you tired, darling?"

"I'm okay," Amanda said.

"Apartment hunting can't be much fun for the kid," Dale said.

"I don't mind," Amanda said. She couldn't tell them she was sad about Pink Pig. She didn't want to hear them say again that she shouldn't still be living in a fantasy world.

"We'll look again on my next leave," Dale said late that afternoon when they were ready to give up for the day. "Let's stop now and grab a bite to eat."

It was the friendly young waitress with the name Betsy on her name tag who steered them to the apartment that Mother liked. They were sitting in the restaurant waiting for their supper order, and Betsy heard

149

them talking about the apartments they'd looked at and not taken.

"My mom has a place to rent," she said as she set down their bread basket. "It's kind of old fashioned, but there's plenty of space and Mom's never jacked the rent up. She just likes having someone share the house with her. It's back of a school. Your little girl could cross the backyard and be there in a minute." She smiled at Amanda. "I guess that's good if you like school."

"I do," Amanda said shyly.

They finished their meal, thanked Betsy, and set off for the apartment. Mother wanted to rent it as soon as she'd walked through the large, clean rooms and been told by the plump, pleasant-faced woman who owned the house that they were welcome to use the garden if they would help her with the watering and weeding. "Some days my arthritis gets me down," she said.

"What do you think?" Mother asked Amanda first.

"Me?" Amanda couldn't believe Mother was consulting her as if she were a person who might have opinions of her own.

"This time I want *you* to be happy," Mother said.

"It looks nice," Amanda said, "And I'd like to water and weed."

The tiny bedroom that was to be hers was under a pitched roof and had no closet, but it faced the school's ball field. Amanda imagined staying after class to help do bulletin boards or shelve books in the library, the kind of things walkers could do because they didn't have to worry about catching a bus. That would be a lot more fun than spending hours alone in an empty apartment every day.

"Well, if you're sure you like it. . . . Good," Mother said with relief. She gave the landlady a deposit on their first month's rent then and there.

Back at Angel's house, everything seemed different. It wasn't home anymore; it was a place they would be leaving soon. Nobody was in the garden. Angel might still be sick in bed, Amanda supposed.

She dreamt Pink Pig was calling to her that night and woke up anxious. But Pink Pig wasn't in the real world anymore, not Amanda's world anyway. The minute Angel got well, Amanda could confront her. "Where's Pink Pig, Angel? What did you do with her?"

Angel's answer would be nasty, no doubt. But if she still had Pink Pig, Amanda would offer her something she wanted. "You're strong," Mother had said. Well, a strong person tried, a strong person might even outwit a bully like Angel.

*   *   *

Monday was a lonely day. Amanda barely spoke to anyone in school. She kept feeling as if she were outside looking in, even on the bus. Back home in the empty apartment, she stood watching the garden, hoping Angel would come into it. She hoped so hard that it surprised her when Angel finally did. Before Amanda could say a word, Angel called to her, "You better come down."

"Why?"

"'Cause I got to talk to you."

"Why should I talk to you? You stole my miniature."

"That's what I want to talk about."

151

Immediately, Amanda hurried down the garage steps and around to the garden gate. "Do you have her?" she asked as Angel let her in.

"Have who?"

"Pink Pig."

Angel opened out her fingers, but when Amanda reached for the miniature, Angel snatched her hand away. "Not so fast. First you got to help me."

"How?"

"I wanna ride that wild horse."

Amanda hid her delight. She did have something Angel wanted, at least the key to something. Coolly, she said, "We'd have to go back to the Little World for that, and to get there I need Pink Pig."

Angel frowned. "Your brother's a troublemaker."

"No, he's not."

"My mom and dad are getting divorced because of him."

"Did you like it with your father, Angel?" Amanda asked out of curiosity.

Angel shook her head. "I ate something bad there that made me sick, and he yelled at me a lot." Her face turned sad. "He kept telling me to go find something to play with, but there wasn't anything. Usually, he's not mean to me, just to my mom."

"So?" Amanda asked after a long silence.

"So, if they get divorced, I don't care." Angel's expression showed she cared very much. "My mom's going to get a job, and I'll have my cousins to play with."

"I'm sorry, Angel," Amanda said. "I mean, about your father."

"Yeah, well, *you* don't even have one."

"No, I don't."

Angel took a big breath and scuffed her sandal on the grass. "Well, but you got a good-looking brother though. He's cute."

"He's a good guy."

"Yeah? Well, so I forgive you."

Amanda tried to think what for, but didn't want to risk making Angel angry by asking.

"Well." Angel abruptly thrust Pink Pig at Amanda. "Here she is. Let's go."

"Amanda!" It was Robbie's excited, happy voice. "Oh, hi, Angel," he added on a downbeat. "I didn't see you. My dad's packing my things up for me. He said I should say good-bye."

"How come you're leaving?" Angel asked.

"We're staying in a motel near the hospital until my mom gets better. Then we're going to find a house. I have to finish up the rest of the math book in the motel while Dad studies Chinese."

"Huh," Angel said. "You're really going? Well, don't expect me to miss you."

Robbie grinned. "That's okay. I won't miss you either."

"I was just going to ask Pink Pig to take us to the Little World," Amanda said. "Angel wants to ride the wild horse."

"Can I come, too?" Robbie asked eagerly.

Amanda nodded. It would be their last trip to the Little World together for a long time, maybe forever. She held Pink Pig to her lips and kissed her lovingly. "Help, Pink Pig," she whispered.

_thirteen

They arrived inside the castle walls where they'd never been before. The courtyard was lined with the folk of the Little World. Peasant Man and Peasant Woman were there, and corn husk girls in their aprons and hats, Peasant Girl with her basket of flowers, even Frog who greeted them with a loud croak. All eyes were fixed on a stage, bare except for an enamel tree. Much more impressive to Amanda's eyes was the high throne next to the great arched door to the stone castle, because on it sat the lady who had been the dark knight. She was dressed in a long white gown with a flower wreath around her head. Her hair flowed to her waist in a black stream, and her hand rested on Brown Knight's shoulder. He sat on a stool beside her.

Brown Knight had spotted them. "Welcome, friends," he called. "You're just in time for the show."

"What show?" Robbie asked.

"Ballerina's new dance. Something about a bird in a

tree. Come on over here and watch with my Dark Lady and me."

"You're not going to battle each other?" Amanda asked. She could see the answer by the way they were leaning toward each other, but she was curious about why they'd become friendly.

Brown Knight didn't mind explaining. "Dark Lady needs help running this kingdom while she's off fighting; so I'm going to be her minister and do a little doctoring on the side."

"But Ballerina—" Amanda blurted out.

Frog had hopped over and settled next to his friend Pink Pig. It was he who spoke. "Ballerina's glad, that Brown Knight isn't sad, that she'll not be his wife, for dancing's her true life."

"Then it's all turned out well," Pink Pig said.

"Very well," Brown Knight said with a grin. "Now I have two beautiful ladies in my life."

"And nobody's going to be eaten?" Amanda asked cautiously.

"We changed the rules." Brown Knight winked. "Everybody gets to do their own thing half a day, and the other half they work, or just look good if that's what they do best. Oh, and Dragon's retiring to the country."

"But where's that wild horse?" Angel asked.

"Out in the field behind the castle last I saw him," Brown Knight said.

Without a word, Angel slipped away.

Amanda looked at Robbie. "Should I go with her? She might get in trouble."

Robbie shrugged. "Angel can take care of herself. Let's stay and watch the show."

A nutcracker soldier blew a fanfare on his trumpet. Through the castle gate came Spangled Giraffe, sequins glittering prettily on his yellow satin hide. He was pulling a painted wooden cart in which Ballerina stood in arabesque position. The crowd held its breath as she was bumped over the cobblestones of the courtyard, but she kept her balance. Spangled Giraffe stopped beside the stage, and Ballerina stood motionless waiting. For what? The puzzle was soon solved. Through the gate came Brass Elephant to lift Ballerina with his trunk and set her lightly down on the stage en pointe. She began to dance to the soft mewing of a violin. Despite all Ballerina's hard labor in the field, she had not lost any of her grace. Her movements were exquisite. For an enchanted while, Amanda watched the bird-in-the-tree dance.

Just as it ended, she heard the sound of hoofbeats. Brown Knight and his Dark Lady looked toward the castle gate. Brown Knight leaped to his feet. "Where's my sword?"

"On the hall table where you left it," Dark Lady said.

"I'll get it," Robbie offered and ran into the castle. Amanda wondered how he was going to find the right hall table, but when she saw who came through the castle gate, she stopped worrying. It was Angel, riding Wild Horse.

"Yippee, yi, yay!" Angel shouted. Everyone pressed back against the walls to give her room. Wild Horse careened around the stage, rearing and bucking. Angel held on, screaming with joy.

"That kid!" Robbie said in disgust. He'd lugged the sword out to the courtyard, but he put it down when he saw Angel. "What a weirdo."

"She's having fun," Pink Pig said.

Amanda thought that she'd never seen Angel look so happy.

She careened around and around the courtyard until Wild Horse finally stopped from exhaustion. He stood shuddering with his head down.

"Did you see that?" Angel asked Amanda. "I told you my dad taught me how to ride."

"I guess he did, Angel," Amanda said.

"I'm going to be a stunt rider someday," Angel said. "Like my daddy was."

The crowd of Little World people began milling aimlessly then as if the highlight event were over. Ballerina was being kissed by both the dark lady and Brown Knight. It looked as if the three had become the best of friends. The rays of the setting sun leaned over the castle wall.

"Whoops!" Robbie said. "I better get back to Angel's garden or my dad's going to wonder what happened to me."

"All right, let's go," Amanda agreed.

Angel parted with Wild Horse reluctantly. Meanwhile, Robbie shook hands with Brown Knight and said how much he'd enjoyed being his companion.

"You're always welcome here, good buddy. You're the man to count on when the going's tough." Brown

Knight slung an arm around Robbie's shoulder affectionately.

Robbie swelled with pride. He shook Brown Knight's hand again and said, "Well, good-bye. I'll come back if you need me."

"Thanks," Brown Knight said, "but it looks like happy-ever-after land here now."

Amanda was just wishing it could be happy-everafter in the real world, too, when suddenly she found herself back in the garden with Angel and Robbie. The sun had left a pink rind above the garden wall, and the sky was milky with evening. Robbie's father stepped out of Angel's house calling, "Robbie, everything's packed. Time to get back to the hospital."

Robbie said a quick good-bye to Angel, then turned his back on her and reminded Amanda, "You're coming to see me soon as my mother's well, and we'll write and call each other. Remember."

"Yes," Amanda said.

"What about me?" Angel asked.

Robbie looked over his shoulder at her in surprise. "You're not my friend," he said, and off he ran to his father.

Angel pouted. "All the games we played in this garden. How come I'm not his friend?"

"Because you weren't nice, Angel. You did terrible, mean things to him."

"Well, what for instance? What was so mean? I just like to kid around is all. He just can't take a joke." She looked hurt enough to cry.

"You beat Robbie up. You hit me," Amanda said.

158

"Well, so. You hit me, too."

Amanda couldn't believe that Angel didn't see herself as she'd appeared to them. Well, Angel had preferred her father to her mother. That showed how blind she was to how people really were. People blindness! How awful not to know who was nice, or even what being nice was.

"Anyway, *you* can come down and play with me," Angel said. "Now Robbie's gone, you don't have a friend."

"Yes, I do." Amanda's fingers tightened around Pink Pig. "Besides, we're going to move soon."

"You're moving, too? How come?"

Without answering that, Amanda said, "Maybe your cousins in Wisconsin will play with you if you don't bully them. I hope so."

Angel didn't say anything.

"Good-bye, Angel," Amanda said. "I'm glad you got to ride Wild Horse. You're a good rider."

Angel shrugged, and still silent, she walked away without looking back.

*　　*　　*

Dale was leaving them that night. Early in the evening, Mother said, "Amanda, you must be so tired. Why don't you go on to bed?"

"I'm not tired, Mother."

Amanda wanted to spend every last minute she could with Dale. But when they were doing the dishes, he whispered to her that he and Mother needed time alone to talk. "It's our only chance, Mouse. You don't mind, do you?"

159

She minded very much, but she was too proud to say so. "I guess I can read in my room," she said.

She took Pink Pig and went off, but she couldn't concentrate on the book. Somehow the murmur of their voices in the living room distracted her—Mother's low laugh, Dale's voice getting louder as he explained something about the girl who'd wanted him to marry her even though he told her he was too young at eighteen to be marrying anybody. Amanda set her book aside. She was suffering from what she'd once called the lonelies.

"I'm tired of being a child," she told Pink Pig.

"You're just mad because they're telling each other things they think you're too young to hear."

"I'm lonely," Amanda complained. "My brother's here and my mother's here and I'm lonely."

"You have me," Pink Pig said.

"Yes, I do," Amanda agreed. "And you'll be my friend forever, won't you?"

"Well, for as long as you want me," Pink Pig promised.

Amanda smiled. That should be long enough, she thought. It would be all right. She had Pink Pig and strength and tomorrow to look forward to. What more could she ask for? Yes, it would be all right. Mother needed her. Mother liked her now. And Dale would come by sometimes. As for Los Angeles—Disneyland was here, and the weather was fine, and maybe there were other good things she could find about it if she looked. She'd look hard, Amanda promised herself, because that was the way to make herself happy here, and she very much liked being happy.